A Desperate Road to Freedom

❈

The Underground Railroad Diary of Julia May Jackson

BY KARLEEN BRADFORD

Scholastic Canada Ltd.

State of Virginia,
United States of America

Saturday, January 10th, 1863

Something is going to happen. I know it! But nobody will tell me anything.

I'm sitting in a corner of Miss Marissa's room in the Big House, scribbling on one of the scraps of paper she gives to me. She's doing her embroidery and I'm just supposed to be keeping her company and running and fetching for her, but once in a while she lets me write, if she's in a good mood. I'm thankful for that, but I can only do it here and I have to be real careful that nobody else sees me. If the Missus found out I could read and write I'd be whipped something fierce. Or worse. Us slaves aren't allowed, but I've been sitting with Miss Marissa during her lessons the whole five years I've been her slave, and I can't help but learn. Seems I pick things up even quicker than her, never mind she's a white girl and I'm only eleven, not twelve like her. I can read better than her, and write better, too. She'd never admit that, of course, even if she does ask for my help sometimes when nobody else is around.

I think Miss Emily, her teacher, suspects that I can read and write, and I think she secretly approves, even though she wouldn't dare say so. Sometimes she looks hard at me when she's explaining something, even when Miss Marissa isn't paying a whit of attention, and gives me a little nod. I mind her good when she does that, even though I pretend I'm not. Figure it's important.

Got to be careful, though. I saw a girl from the next cabin over whipped when they found out she could read just a couple of words, and I still have nightmares about it. I keep seeing her back all cut and bleeding and getting bloodier and bloodier with every stroke of the cowhide. She screamed at first, then she just sort of collapsed. The overseer didn't stop though, not him. Just kept on whipping and whipping until her skin was hanging off in strips. I swear he enjoyed it. He had a mean little smile going all the time he was doing it. She was sold off at the slave auction right after and I never saw her again.

But I'm afraid about more than that. Mama is going around with her face all tight and squinched up and her mouth latched shut. I haven't seen her so afflicted since the Master sold off Caleb and Daniel and Sarah. Papa won't even look at me, and Thomas just about took my head off this morning over noth-ing at all. Little Joseph's the only one acting normal, but that's just because he's so young.

What is going on? My stomach is just plain sour with worry.

Monday, January 12th, 1863

I'm putting the date on the top of my writing like Miss Marissa does with her lessons. Miss Marissa didn't want me to stay over tonight in the Big House, so I snuck my paper back to the cabin with me and found a hidey-hole behind the chimney where I can stash it. She only lets me have scraps that she's messed up and doesn't want any more, but I can still write on the back of them. Keeping a stub of a pencil there, too.

It's dangerous, what I'm doing. Can't even let Mama know. She'd have my hide and throw the papers in the fire for sure. She wouldn't understand. Don't really understand myself why the writing's so important to me, but it is. Especially now when everybody's acting so strange.

Tuesday, January 13ᵗʰ, 1863

Something terrible happened last night. I was woken up by dogs howling and baying, and men shouting, then I heard noises that sounded like shots. I don't know what went on, but nobody's talking. I tried to ask Papa and he just shushed me up. The hands going out to the fields this morning weren't singing the way they usually do. They just shuffled out, their faces all grim and their mouths shut tight.

Don't dare write any more. Got to hide these pages real good. Things are happening that I don't understand.

Wednesday, January 14ᵗʰ, 1863

Well, I know now what happened the other night and I wish I didn't. Bessie's papa, Uncle Bo, tried to make free and they caught him. Shot him dead. Mama and Papa still aren't telling me anything, but I heard Mama trying to console Auntie Sal. Even though Uncle Bo isn't my real uncle, I still feel bad about it.

Thursday, January 15th, 1863

Heard something else about Uncle Bo, but it makes me feel so sick I don't even want to think about it. Maybe if I write it down I can get rid of it. I heard Auntie Sal tell Mama they've got Uncle Bo's body hanging from the big old hickory tree by the plantation gate. An example to the rest of us, she said. In case anybody else was of a mind to run. She was repeating my Mama's name, "Selie, Selie," over and over, and crying so hard I could barely make out what she was saying.

With the war between the North and the South going on, and that Northern President Lincoln wanting all the slaves in the Confederate states here in the South to be free, slaves are running away more and more. Our Master's off fighting and nobody's tending this plantation too well. We've even heard gunshots and fighting right close around here. I suppose that's why Uncle Bo thought he had a chance.

Friday, January 16th, 1863

Mama's so twitchy she slapped Joseph. That's not like her at all. Joseph's going around whimpering, but not even Thomas is paying him any mind. And that's not like Thomas, either. Spite of everything, Thomas usually has a smile and a joke in him for Joseph and me, but not now.

There's more going on than just grieving for Uncle Bo, I know it!

_____

WE'RE RUNNING!

_____

Not sure what day it is. I lost track.

_____

I can't believe we're running and we got away! So far.

_____

I got my scraps of paper and pencil with me, tucked down the front of my shift, and a rope tied tight around my middle to keep them safe. Wasn't going to go without them. Writing when everybody's asleep, though it's barely light enough to see my pages.

I'm scared!

Too many strange noises outside.

I keep thinking it's the slave catchers with their dogs.

Hands shaking too much to write anything else.

———————

Still don't know what day it is, but I can write more now. We're hiding in a barn. I had to wait till Mama and Papa and Thomas went to sleep before I could start, because I don't want anybody to know what I'm doing. This is the first chance I've had to collect myself and set down what's happened. I still can't really believe it!

Seems Thomas heard tell they were going to sell him off, too, so he and Mama and Papa fixed to run. They didn't dare say a word about what they were planning to do, especially after Uncle Bo got caught. Mama said they nearly backed out then, but the thought of losing Thomas was just too much to bear so they decided to go ahead and take the chance, terrible though it was. Mama said she would die if she lost another one of her children.

I was too young to remember much about when

my brothers Caleb and Daniel were sold off, but I do remember when they took our Sarah. We didn't even know she'd been sold until the overseer, Mister Jones, came busting into our cabin and grabbed hold of her one morning after Papa had left for his work in the stables and Thomas had left for the fields. "Master got a good price for this gal," he said, and started to drag her out.

Sarah let out a shriek and reached for Mama. Mama caught her and held on tight, but Mister Jones just yanked her away. Sarah was doing her best to keep hold of Mama, and Mama was crying and trying to hang onto her, but he pulled her out the door. When Mama rushed after them, another man pushed her back so hard she fell down. I was standing in the corner and watching the whole thing. I will never forget it. Couldn't move. I was just froze with fear, but I remember I screamed out to them to leave my big sister alone. Didn't do a mite of good. They took her off and we never saw her again. Don't even know who they sold her to, but it couldn't have been anybody around here or we would have heard.

I know Mama and Papa are afraid Sarah and Caleb and Daniel were sold off to work in the cotton fields away down south. We'll never hear more about them if they were. Even worse there than on a tobacco plantation like ours. Stories we hear say that slaves don't last long down there. Work's too hard and they die. I can't bear thinking of it.

I still miss Sarah and I always will.

I reckon Mama and Papa didn't say a word about running because they couldn't count on Joseph to keep from talking, but I'm hurt that they didn't trust *me*. First thing I knew about it, Mama was shaking me awake in the middle of the night, with her hand pressed over my mouth so I wouldn't cry out or make a noise when I woke up.

"Hush, Julia May!" she whispered at me. It was dead cold and she was all bundled up. She made me put on every scrap of clothes I owned, not that I have much, just my shift and a shirt and an old jacket that Miss Marissa gave me when she didn't have any more use for it. All the while Mama was hissing at me to be quiet, but in spite of her rushing me, I hung back after she left the cabin and that's how come I got my papers and pencil out. Papa was already outside with Joseph asleep in his arms and Thomas looking out, scared like. They were all bundled up, too, but shivering with the cold just as bad as me. It wasn't just the cold, though. I knew what was happening so the shivering was from fear, too.

We snuck behind the cabins and made for the trees. Mama and Papa had waited until there wasn't a moon, so it was real dark. Middle of the night dark. I had to hang onto Mama's skirts so as not to lose her. I heard an owl hoot somewhere and that scared me even more, but Papa just tilted his head to listen and then beckoned us.

Once we got deep into the trees, there was a Negro lady waiting there for us. She had a walking stick in one hand and a bundle over her shoulder. Couldn't see her too well in the dark, but she sort of waved the stick at us. "Follow me," she whispered. "And hush your mouths good!"

I shut my mouth but my heart was beating so hard I was sure you could hear it right up to the Big House. We followed her for the longest time. It was hard walking. I'd never walked in between the trees before and I kept tripping over roots and branches. I fell twice. The first time no one even noticed and I had to pick myself up quick and catch up with the others. I guess I was crying a bit, because Thomas hung back a little and grabbed my hand. The next time I tripped he caught me and pulled me up. He kept good hold of my hand from then on and that made me feel better. We none of us said a word, but I could hear Mama breathing hard. Once Joseph started to whimper, but Papa just turned Joseph's face into his chest and muffled his noise. I was afraid he'd smother him, but it seemed to make Joseph feel better. Enough that he stopped his cry-ing, anyway.

Then we heard the dogs!

Joseph's fussing again right now. I'd better go to him. I'll write about the dogs soon as I get another chance.

It's barely light enough to see my pages, but I can manage.

Joseph was having a bad dream. I don't wonder after what happened that day. He might be only five years old and not sure what's going on, but he knows enough to be scared. I got him settled back down before any of the others woke up, but then I couldn't sleep. Too many pictures in my head that I didn't want to see.

When we heard the dogs we all froze. Then the lady grabbed us and pulled us into some thick bushes and we huddled there, all holding onto each other. The bushes prickled something awful, but we none of us paid them any mind at all. We heard the dogs coming closer and closer, baying and howling just the way they were the night Uncle Bo got caught. Men were shouting, too. The noise was fierce and it was coming straight at us. I held my breath and prayed as hard as I could. I knew real well those dogs could smell us easy as could be in those bushes. All I could think of was Uncle Bo shot and hanging dead in that tree.

When it seemed they were right about to crash into us, I started to cry. Couldn't help it. I was so scared I even wet myself. Just as I closed my eyes and waited to feel those teeth tearing into me, I heard the dogs run past. Right *past* us! And then it sounded like they went crazy.

"They got him!" someone cried. At the same time, I heard a man scream. The man screamed again. And again. I never in my life heard anything so terrible. I heard a shot, and the screaming stopped. That quiet was even worse than the screaming.

We stayed huddled there together while the men called to the dogs, and went off, laughing and joking. Joseph was hanging tight to Papa and wouldn't even look up. Papa kept soothing him and rubbing his back, telling him things were all right. Finally, the lady signalled to us to stay hidden while she made certain they had all gone. When she came back, she beckoned to us to follow her.

"Safe now," she said.

But I don't think I'll ever feel safe again.

We walked all night. By the time the sun started peeking down through the trees I was so tired I was leaning hard on Thomas. Just when I thought I couldn't go one step farther, the lady stopped so quick we all nearly bumped into her. She told us to stay put, then she disappeared. Mama and Papa got worried, but she came right back and waved at us to follow her again. She led us out of the woods and across a little stump-filled sort of garden. There was a log cabin there, with a single candle burning in the window. A quilt hung over the porch railings and flapped a little in the morning breeze — somebody must have been home — but there wasn't a sign of anybody around. The lady led us to a chicken coop at the back. I couldn't believe it when she whispered to us to go in there!

It was horrible! Chickens all around, the stink was something awful. Then she whispered that we had to stay in there all day till it got dark again and she left us.

That was a truly terrible day. I swear those chickens hated us. They stared at us with nasty, beady little eyes and pecked anyone who came anywhere near them. We all just scrunched ourselves into one corner and tried to keep out of their way. We were tired to the bone but there was no sleeping in there. Besides, though we didn't say a word about it, we none of us could forget what had happened in the woods. I knew what Mama and Papa and Thomas were thinking. It could happen to *us*. Any time. Easy as anything.

A lady came in to collect eggs after a while, but she made like she didn't see us. She was a Negro lady, too, but she looked like a farmer's wife. She and her husband must have been free Negroes. Papa told me some do manage to make enough money to buy their freedom if they've got good masters who let them work for other people. Not our Master, though. He's too mean.

We pretended we didn't see her, either. She got two eggs and then opened the coop door to let the chickens out. I thought she was going to say something then, but she didn't. She just gave us a look and made a kind of soothing motion with her hand, then went out herself and closed the door again.

We didn't see anybody else for the rest of the day. The smell and the chicken dirt were pretty bad, but at least the chickens were gone. Joseph started playing around with the feathers and Mama started to fuss at him about the dirt on them, then stopped. I figure she was just glad to see him getting somewhere back to his usual self.

We ran again soon as it was dark, and the next day we hid in a barn. That's what we do, travel all night and then hide all day somewhere. The lady who helped us get away — she wouldn't tell us her name — calls herself a Conductor. Seems we're on a railroad! Underground Railroad she calls it. It's not a real railroad, though. Just one safe place after another. Today we're hiding in a white Quaker lady's shed. Our Conductor told us that Quakers are people whose religion doesn't believe in slavery. Sounds like a good religion to me.

We're in a barn again today. Walked all night and I am tired right down to my bones and freezing cold. Joseph couldn't walk at all, so Thomas carried him.

Thomas must be tired because he's lying flat on his back and snoring up a storm now. Joseph's curled up in his arms and snoring too, like a little echo.

We're headed for Fortress Monroe, our Conductor says. It's a Union Army fort, right here in Virginia. It's on the coast and it sticks right out into the ocean. The Union Army fortifide it on the land side and that's how they managed to keep the Confederate Army from capturing it. Don't know if that's how to spell *fortifide*. It's a new word for me. Heard Thomas say it.

Thomas is real interested in army stuff so he was asking all sorts of questions about the Fortress, and I listened as hard as I could. They're taking in escaped slaves there and calling them "contrabands of war." The general at the Fortress says because Virginia seeseeded from the United States and is fighting on the Confederate side now, he's got no call to send escaped slaves back to their masters. Our Conductor says there are hundreds of slaves getting shelter there. They call it the Freedom Fortress.

I asked her how to spell *seeseeded* and she looked at me strange. I realized just in time that I shouldn't be asking things like that so I shut my mouth up quick and I'm guessing how to spell it. Didn't dare ask her how to spell *fortifide* either.

I'll see the ocean! Wonder what it's like.

In a shed again today. Rain coming in through the roof. Snow, too. Never been so cold and wet in my life. Our cabin back at the plantation was small, but it was better than this. We at least had a hearth there where we could make a fire to keep warm, and a wood floor, and Papa kept the roof fixed good so it wouldn't leak. The floor here is mud right up to my ankles, mixed up with all kinds of dirt. I didn't want to lie down in that muck and I guess I whined about it. Next I knew, Mama gave me a good slap on the back of the head and told me to hush up and lie down on the scrap of cloth she put out for me. Look on her face — I did it and did it fast. Didn't like it though. Heard some dogs barking and that got me thinking scared again. Everybody else is asleep, so I tucked myself into a corner to write. There's no windows in the shed, though, just a little crack in the wall, and I can't really see too well, so I'm going to stop.

Can't get to Fortress Monroe. There's fighting right between us and the Fortress. We've been hearing the guns all day while we're hiding. Our Conductor says she'll take us to the Great Dismal Swamp instead and we can wait there till the fighting dies down and it's safe to go on. That's a scary name, but Papa has heard of it and he says lots of escaped slaves are living in there and they'll take care of us. The guns and noise make me want to hide my head under a pillow. Haven't got a pillow, though.

I wonder how Bessie is doing. I spent most of my time up in the Big House with Miss Marissa, but I did like to sit in the evenings sometimes with Bessie and listen to Uncle Bo play the mouth organ. His songs were often kind of sad, but I liked them anyway. He taught me to sing some with him, too. Said I had a right nice voice. I miss him, but probably not near as much as Bessie and her mama do. I still can't think of what happened to him without a sick, horrible feeling in my stomach.

I wonder what Bessie thought when she realized we got away? Wonder if she thought I had abandoned her?

Mama is stirring. Got to hide these pages away now.

Friday, January 23rd, 1863

Can't hardly believe it, but we've made it to Fortress Monroe, the Freedom Fortress! And I know what day it is.

Actually, we're not right inside the Fortress, but in a kind of camp just outside of it, on account of how many runaways have taken shelter here, and there are too many to fit in the Fortress itself. They call this the Grand Contraband Camp.

There's nothing very grand about it, though. There are so many people here we just got a corner of a cabin for ourselves and we share with another family. Other family's name is Ross. There's a mama and a papa and four children, all younger than me. Makes the cabin kind of crowded, but it's still better than the chicken coops and barns we've been hiding in.

Some white ladies here from something called the American Missionary Association took us in when we got here. I know how to spell that because the name is written on the packs they carried with them. They showed us where we could live, even gave us some clothes and little bags with a towel, a comb, a bar of soap and a toothbrush in each one of them. A toothbrush! Imagine! Don't know anybody other than

Miss Marissa who ever had a special brush just for their teeth. They even gave Joseph one and he immediately started in to brushing his hair with it until I made him stop and showed him how to use it proper. I got a clean dress. It's got a few rips in it, but it's got red flowers on it and it's pretty. A lot nicer than that itchy linsey-woolsey shift Missus Jackson gave me to wear. And they gave me a warm coat. I do appreciate that! Marissa's old jacket is pretty thin. We got food, too.

They got a school here for us colored people — children and grown-ups. Teach them to write. I had to bite my tongue when she told us that, not to let on that I already knew how. Maybe they won't let me go if they know.

We were so happy until one of the ladies started in on warning us about slave catchers. Seems we should be safe here, but because we're outside the walls of the Fortress, the soldiers can't keep good track of who gets into the camp. Some slave catchers got in about a month ago and grabbed a man. Got him out before anyone could call up the soldiers. Mama didn't like the sound of that at all, but Papa says we'll be fine. Hope he's right. I don't even want to think about what would happen if they caught us and carried us back to our Master. We'd all be whipped, that's certain, except maybe for Joseph. He's too little. Surely they wouldn't whip him. But they might even hang Papa or Thomas like they hung Uncle Bo!

Another worry was that Mama, Papa and Thomas had to find work and earn some money, but there are so many runaways here that there aren't many jobs to be had for new people. We can't keep on taking stuff for free, though, no matter how kind the Missionary ladies are. There's a market here on Saturdays where people sell vegetables they grow, and all kinds of other things, and we have to be able to buy what we need. Believe it or not, Joseph solved the problem. Not that he meant to, though.

That boy is always up to something — usually trouble — and this time it was no different. He snuck off when I wasn't watching him and decided to go across the bridge over to the Fortress. Course he's not supposed to do that at all, and of course he fell off. First thing we knew of it, a soldier brought him, all dripping wet, back to the cabin. Mama was fit to be tied and Papa was all set to give him a good licking, but the soldier, name of Ben, just laughed and begged Papa not to. Said he'd fished Joseph out with no trouble at all — he'd just fallen down into the shallow water between the wall and the shore, and Ben hadn't even got more than his boots wet getting Joseph out. Papa relented, but now I'm in trouble for not keeping a better watch on him. That isn't one bit fair.

Anyway, Thomas got to talking to Ben and seems like they hit it off real good, even though Ben's a white boy. Next thing we knew, Ben had fixed it so that Mama got some washing to do for him and some of his friends and Papa got a job helping out in the stables on account of he worked with horses back at the plantation and he's got a way with them. Ben took him down to the stables to see about getting some work there and Papa calmed down a mare so nervous she wouldn't let anybody else near her. The captain there was real impressed.

Mama got to be a fine laundress from all the washing and ironing she did at the Big House, so she's pleased to have work here, too. Thomas keeps busy doing whatever little job comes up with the soldiers, even if it's just running errands and taking messages, and he earns a bit of money that way.

I've seen the ocean now. I never knew there could be so much space just dedicated to water! I stood on the shore staring and staring at all those waves moving in and moving out until I got as spellbound as a mouse about to be gobbled up by a snake. Water's full of salt. That's true. You can't drink it at all. Imagine that!

Even though I was supposed to stay and mind Joseph, and I didn't want to get into any more trouble, I managed to get away long enough to find a place to write all this out. The words were just filling me up until I had to get them set down or bust. Joseph made friends with the little boy from the family we're sharing with, named Abe, and Missus Ross said she'd mind him, so I've been out exploring around. Keeping a pert look-out for slave catchers.

Found myself a huge big tree just made for climbing and sitting in and that's where I am now. Leaves hide me and nobody can see me. Because he knows I'm going to go to school, Thomas got me an old scribbler, thanks to his friend Ben again. It's been used before, but there's still lots of room left to write in it.

First off I'll write about the Great Dismal Swamp.

We got there in the dark of night. Our Conductor handed us over to the biggest colored man I've ever seen in my life. He was just huge. Had a mass of grey hair and a great, bushy white beard — looked like a big bear looming up there in the darkness, but he spoke gentle. Told us to follow exactly in his footsteps, otherwise we might fall into the swamp and drown. He was right, too. I slipped a bit and went into slimy, cold water right up to my knees. Papa hauled me out quick and I was more careful after that. So cold, though, I couldn't help shivering. And *scared*. I heard owls hooting and other slithery noises that I didn't even want to think about. Worse even than dogs. I asked if there were any snakes there and the man just laughed. "Lots of snakes, girl," he said. "You just keep close behind me."

The trees hung over us and closed us in on all sides. Running through the woods was bad enough, but you couldn't run in that swamp, there were too many vines and tree roots and bushes. Pretty well had to fight our way through them. I was sure the vines were snakes and worried they might jump down on me, but the man just laughed again. Said no snake was going to fall on me out of a tree. Bite my ankle more like. I walked even closer to him than before. Mama followed me, then Thomas carrying Joseph, and Papa came on behind. Thomas kept stumbling and I was scared he'd fall, but he managed. Don't know what we'd do without Thomas.

Can't write any more. Hear Mama calling. She sounds provoked. I better hightail it back.

Saturday, January 24th, 1863

I was afraid Joseph had got into mischief again, but thank the good Lord he hadn't. Mama just wanted me to help with the washing. Got some more time to myself now. Joseph and Abe are playing and Missus Ross doesn't let them out of her sight for one moment. It's good of her to do that, because Abe's a little imp just like Joseph and the two of them together are a handful. I'm up in my tree. So funny. People walk right by under me and got no idea a girl is sitting up here high above them.

Missionary lady says I can start going to the school next week. My stomach is all twisty with the thought of it. But for now I'll go on with my story.

We finally got into a kind of camp, way deep in the swamp. The man showed us a tarp stretched between two trees to make a kind of shelter and we huddled there. It was awful cold. We none of us slept that night, but next morning the man — never did find out his name — built up a fire for us. While we were warming ourselves, two other men came out of the trees with a bucket of catfish. They fried them up over the fire and shared them with us. I was so hungry by then that those fish tasted better than anything I ever ate in my life. Fried crispy brown and dripping with grease — oh, my stomach is cramped up just thinking about them.

We stayed there all the next day and I forgot to be scared and almost got to enjoying myself. The camp was on a kind of island with swampy water on most sides of us and there were so many birds. I loved watching them. One of them was singing real pretty. There were other shanties around us and about fifteen or twenty people living there. No other children, though. The people were kindly, but sort of holding back. Guess they knew we were just sheltering there for a bit and would soon be moving on. Not like them. They're escaped slaves who have chosen to live in there rather than try to get to the Fortress. Free spirits, Papa calls them. Suits them, I suppose, but it must be a hard life. I heard someone moaning in the shack next to us and a woman came out looking worried. When I asked what was the matter, she just hardly looked at me and muttered "snake bit." I didn't ask more. I most decidedly wouldn't want to live there.

We left that night and got here to the Fortress two days later. I'll write more about how it is here tomorrow. Time to get back now.

Sunday, January 25th, 1863

Today's the Sabbath, so we went to church this morning. There's a little chapel inside the Fortress. I saw it when I climbed up on the walls, but that's just for the soldiers and the white folks. A minister from the American Missionary Association holds services for us Contrabands in the school here. It doesn't feel much like a church, and the service was sort of boring, but we gave thanks for reaching safety, anyway. We truly do have a lot to be thankful for. I said a special prayer for Caleb and Daniel and Sarah. It's hard to let ourselves be happy here when we don't know where they are or what's happened to them.

There wasn't much singing, and I like singing, but I got to look around the school and imagine what it will be like when I go there. It's just one big room with benches all along the edges. A table at the front. The Missionary minister stood there today, but I reckon the teacher stands up there when they're using it as a school. There's a big blackboard up behind the table. Guess they write on that with chalk. There was something written on it, but it had been scrubbed out and I couldn't make out what it said. A big cupboard on one side, and a big round sort of ball with colored markings on it on a stand beside the table. The floor was scrubbed so clean it looked almost white.

I can't believe I'm going to be able to go to school there! I can't wait! I wonder if they got books in that cupboard. I would love to read a book all the way through from front to back. Marissa had books, but she never bothered much with them. I wasn't allowed to touch them, but sometimes I got peeks at what was in them before she closed them up. It was like having a candy sweet held out in front of me, then snatched away.

Back to my story.

The night we left that Great Dismal Swamp, one of the men from the camp led us back to the edge of the swamp and another man was waiting for us there. Said he was our new Conductor. He carried us here to the Fortress. We travelled at night and sheltered in sheds and barns as usual during the day. Got here in the middle of the night, cold and miserable. It was snowing hard.

I am so happy to be here. Our little cabin may be crowded, but we got a fire and it's warmer than being out in the woods under a tarp.

❈

Monday, January 26ᵗʰ, 1863

I shouldn't have written that last bit. We aren't staying! Just when we got somewhere safe, after all that running, we aren't staying! Mama's fretting and even Papa's worried, and not just about the slave catchers. Thomas doesn't talk about anything but the soldiers and the war and the battles that are going on all around us. We are the only Union Army fortress this far south and we are surrounded by the Confederate forces, he says. Seems to get him all excited to think of it. He even said he wished he could fight like the soldiers. But Papa is afraid they will attack this Fortress and what will happen then? If they take it, we'll all be sent back to our masters and we know what they will do to us. Mama and he talked all night last night and we're going to run again. This time, Papa says, we're going all the way to a place called Canada. That's another country altogether, away up to the north, where everybody is free. No slaves at all! No slave catchers! Can't imagine that.

Thomas says he can arrange for another Conductor to meet us and carry us there. That Underground Railroad we were on goes all the way up, he says. The soldiers told him so. We'll be running again, and there will be dogs . . .

I don't want to go! I even made a big fuss about it — something I hardly ever do. I cried and stomped my feet until Mama got angry with me. Didn't make a whit of difference. We're going anyway.

I won't be going to school. Knew it was too good to be true. And it's going to be dangerous to write again. If I even get a chance. I don't want to get anybody else in trouble, and they would be if these papers were ever found, but I NEED to write.

We're running again. Just like before. Worse though, because we were safe for a while and it felt so good. We've been running and running. Nothing to do but move on at night and sleep in barns or sheds during the day, and eat whatever scraps our new Conductor finds for us.

Yesterday we had to sleep out under the trees and it was terrible. Rained hard, with some snow in it. The clothes the ladies in Fortress Freedom gave us are getting ragged and our shoes are nearly worn out. I do appreciate that coat, though. I've fallen down so many times I can't count how many bruises I have on my arms and legs. Joseph stumbled into the branch of a tree and he got a huge big welt all down one side of his face. We were near freezing to death, but that wasn't the worst of it. Out there, with no walls around us, I expected to be pounced on by some kind of wild animal any minute. I snuggled up to Joseph and held him so tight he squirmed away and told me to let him be. Felt so scary, being out in the daylight. We were hid good, but I kept expecting someone to discover us.

Our Conductor found us a barn to sleep in today, but I'm going to write this down first. Mama and Papa and Thomas fall to sleep soon as they lie down, so does Joseph, but I can't. Keep thinking and thinking about things. Just after we left Fortress Freedom we passed a burned-out plantation. The house shone white in the dark, but when we got close we saw it was all burned-out inside. Vines already starting to grow around it and the garden was full of weeds. It was so quiet and lonely looking. Spooked us all. Wonder where the folks that used to live there are now? Wonder where their slaves are? Wonder what's happening to everybody back at our plantation?

We had to cross a big river on a raft. We all got soaking wet and it was scary. The night was calm and quiet — good for the crossing on that rickety old raft, but not good so far as making noise was concerned. Our Conductor warned us not to make a sound, and we didn't, but I was sure someone would hear the noise of our paddle. Lucky our Conductor is a big strong man and he got us across quick.

I fell down again today while we were climbing up a hill covered in loose, scraggly rock. Skinned both knees right over some old scabs that had just started to heal, and they bled all down into my shoes. Mama bandaged them up when we got here with some old rags, but I got so many hurts now, a few more don't make any difference. We all do, so there's no use making a fuss about it. Mama's feet are so blistered she can't wear her shoes, just fixes more rags around her feet and keeps her shoes tied by their strings around her neck. She never says a word about the pain, so I figure I can hush my mouth about my bruises, too.

I hate this! Mama is so thin her eyes look like they're staring out of her head. Thomas and Papa's faces are so grim their mouths are just solid lines, and their eyes are wary all the time. Looking round, trying to see everything at once. Little Joseph has stopped talking. That's not like him. He's just getting quieter and quieter and skinnier and skinnier. Hardly anything left of him at all.

Something bad happened yesterday. We were handed over to another Conductor, and he was an older man. Sort of frail. Mama fussed at him because she thought he was too old to be doing this sort of thing, but he just fussed right back at her. Said he'd been a slave himself and was helped by the Underground Railroad to escape, and he was going to keep on helping others till he dropped.

We were going down a steep hill and next we knew, he stepped on a loose stone and fell. He tried to get up again, but he couldn't. Mama said his leg was broke for sure. He told us to go on and told us where to go, but no way were Mama and Papa going to leave him. We didn't know what to do, but Thomas just scooped him up and said he'd carry him. Thomas is real big, and the Conductor was pretty spare, but it still was a heavy burden. Thomas was set on it, though. Nobody can be as determined as Thomas when he puts his mind to a thing, so for the rest of the night he carried that old man on his back.

The man was moaning with pain and after a bit he fainted, but Thomas figured out the way to go and we knew what house to look for. Soon enough we saw it. It was a white man's house, but there was a quilt hanging over the porch railing, just like the old man said there would be. We hid in the barn while Thomas carried the Conductor up to the steps. We peeked out through the barn door, watching. I knew Mama and Papa were thinking same as me. What if it's the wrong house? We were none of us breathing when Thomas knocked quiet on the door. It opened and a white man looked out. Seemed like he just stood there forever, looking at Thomas without saying a word, then he nodded and motioned Thomas to take the Conductor in. Soon Thomas came back out to the barn, carrying a poke full of crackers and cheese.

Thomas told us the white man and his wife said they'd take care of the Conductor. See that he got to a doctor. There'd be another Conductor to take us on tonight, they said. The man and his wife thanked Thomas for carrying the Conductor to them. Said he was a truly good man and deserved it.

Makes me feel good inside to know that we could give back some of the help we've been getting all these weeks.

———————

Fighting all around us. We didn't dare move last night because we were afraid there were still soldiers in the area. Just laid real low.

———————

I lost track of time again. I just remember waking up sometimes, all in a sweat because I was sure I heard dogs. Once we really did. That night we didn't run, we just stayed put in another barn. The owner of the house was a white lady.

———————

Our Conductor — another Negro lady now — showed us the stars last night and pointed out a bunch that look just like a drinking gourd tilted down. She said that if you draw a line from the two stars on the front of it upwards, you'll see a really bright star. That's the north star and that's what we have to follow to take us north to freedom. To Canada.

I remember Sarah always singing a song about following the drinking gourd. I used to sing along with her although I never did know what it meant. Now I know what the words were saying.

I suppose I shouldn't be writing that down, case somebody does catch us, but if they do I'll bury these pages quick or mess them up so good nobody can read them. Writing things down is the only comfort I got.

I wonder if Sarah got a chance to run and follow that star? Maybe she's already free. In Canada. She was such a good big sister to me and I loved her so much — I want to believe she's some place where she can be happy.

Going through Pennsylvania. That sure is a hard word to spell, but I think I got it right. We are all too tired now even to talk.

How much longer is this going to go on? Don't know how much more I can take. Don't know how much more any of us can take.

Think it's March now. Not sure.

Still raining, but no more snow, thank goodness.

We're nearly in New York State, but we've got mountains to go around. I can see them in the distance. Glad we don't have to go over them. We've been climbing enough hills. Our Conductor says we've got to follow the Hudson River Valley up to near Albany, then we turn west and follow the Mohawk Valley to a town called Rochester. She's going to see that we get on a Canadian steamer there to carry us over to the other side of the lake, and that's Canada.

I don't understand any of it. Just wish we were back in the Freedom Fortress.

————————————

Our Conductor tells us we're in New York State now. Finally.

————————————

Friday, April 3rd, 1863

We made it to Albany. Hiding in the root cellar of a stone house on a big river called the Hudson. We've all had a chance to rest up a bit. White lady lives here and she brought us a dinner of fried stripers like you wouldn't believe. We couldn't even eat it all. Even better than catfish. Got some saved for tomorrow when we'll be off again. Joseph stuffed himself so much I thought he'd be sick, but he's got life back in his eyes and he even smiled at me. He's curled up sleeping now and snoring like a happy hound dog.

They mostly call us colored up here in the north, not Negroes. Makes no matter to me what they call us, though. I know who I am.

All the colored folk around here are free. No slavery allowed in New York State, but we still got to hide because of something called the Fujitiv Slave Law. I'm just guessing at how to spell *fujitiv*. Never had any call to write that word down before.

That law says that if anybody up here finds an escaped slave, they got to send him back south. Free colored people here got to carry their free papers with them all the time because slave catchers come up here looking for runaways and carry them back south. Sometimes they grab folks they know are free and kidnap them anyway, papers or not.

I snuck out of the root cellar early this morning. Couldn't stand being shut in the dark anymore and had to get out. That's where I'm writing now. The sun is just coming up and there are swallows flitting through the air, catching flies coming up from the water. Ducks bobbing all around, too. It's all so peaceful and quiet. I would dearly love to live somewhere like this place and not have to be afraid of anything.

Better get back down to the root cellar now, though.

Friday, April 10th, 1863

We got to Rochester. Tired. We've been on the run all night every night to get here. Rochester is on a lake so big I can't see the end of it. Can't believe it's more than two months since we left the Freedom Fortress. But, some ways, it seems more like two years.

We're hiding out in a free colored family's barn. They can go anywhere they want! Thomas says that after this war, if the Northern States win it, all the colored people in the country will be free and will be able to live like that. Can't believe it. Mama doesn't believe it, either. She still says we got to get out of here while the getting is good.

Saturday, April 11th, 1863

Man who owns this place — we aren't given their names, just in case — knows which Canadian captains are willing to take runaways over to Canada. He says that slave catchers keep watch over the harbor and check that all the colored people getting on the boats have free papers, but since the war started they're not around so much. He says that if he keeps watch he can let us know when it's safe for us to go.

The man's wife came out to the barn today with new clothes for all of us, so we'll look respectable when we get to Canada. Well, not new, but clean. We need them. The clothes the Missionary ladies gave us at Fortress Monroe are hanging in tatters. I even got new boots that are only a little bit too big for me. I expect I will grow into them. They've been worn a lot, so they're already nice and soft.

We're all so nervous, though, we don't even want to talk. Just hiding here, waiting.

Friday, April 17th, 1863

Dark of the moon. If there's no slave catchers on the dock tonight, the man says we're going. His wife is a nice lady. She brought us a hot supper. She said they wouldn't feed us on the boat and we'd best eat hearty before we set out, but my stomach was so tied up in knots I couldn't eat a bite. I think Mama and Papa felt just about the same, but they didn't want to hurt her feelings so they forced it down. Only ones who could eat their fill were Thomas and Joseph. Thomas never refuses food and Joseph does whatever Thomas does.

Saturday, April 18th, 1863

We're on the boat! I'm scrunched in a corner down below the main deck. Can't hardly write, the boat is rolling around so much. Mama is up on the deck. She's sick from the rolling. So are Thomas and Jacob and Papa. Doesn't seem to bother me none, but maybe it's just as well I didn't eat supper.

It was scary getting on board. The man who was hiding us carried us to the harbor and we hid in some trees while he scouted it out to make sure there weren't any slave catchers around. It was pitch dark with no moon at all and there were only a few lights on the boats that were tied up in there, but there was a lighthouse. It shot out a great beam of light that turned around and around up at the top of it and lit everything up. Every time it did, we just shuddered back into the shadows. There was a big old iron bridge there, too, that crossed the harbor. It looked spooky when the light shone on it. The man pointed out the boat we were going to go on, then he just sort of melted into the darkness. There was a plank leading down from the side of it to the shore, but I couldn't see anybody around. Suddenly he was back.

"Hurry up," he whispered to us. "Up that plank with you. Go through the door at the top and down below. Hunker down there and don't make a sound."

We didn't hardly have time to thank him. He was a free man, but if he'd been found helping slaves he would have been in a passel of trouble. Don't think being free would help him one bit. It's against the law to help escaped slaves, even up here in the North. Specially for colored people. Figure he'd be punished as much as we would if they caught him. He's a right brave man. So is his wife. And so is that old man who broke his leg helping us. Wouldn't be surprised if he's back on the Railroad soon as his leg's mended.

Makes me think about all the people who helped us. Thomas says it takes courage to run like we did, but it takes courage for people to help us like they did, too. Even white people. Papa says white people who help slaves escape get fined a lot of money and thrown in jail! We got a powerful lot to be grateful for. Not likely we could do this without them.

After the man left us, we snuck up the plank, quiet as we could. There weren't any sailors around at all. Then we slid through a door that had been left open, climbed down a ladder, and hid below the deck. We stayed down there all night. This morning we heard sailors shouting and the engine started up with a roar and a clanking that near scared the wits right out of me. I just crouched there with my hands over my ears. Next thing we knew, we could feel the boat moving and we knew we were on our way. After a while a sailor came down and said we could go up on the deck if we wanted. He was a white man, but he treated us real respectful.

Going to tuck this back down safe in my dress and go up. Want to see what it looks like up there. Want to stand out in the open in the broad daylight and feel the wind in my face. Wind of freedom, that's what it is.

Tomorrow we'll be in Canada.

TORONTO, CANADA!

We made it! We're here, safe and sound! We were met the moment we got off the boat by the kindliest preacher I've ever known. He gathered us up and carried us to his home. He's been free all his life — imagine that. His missus gave us a good hot meal, more clean almost-new clothes, and then let us sleep in soft beds with white sheets! I think I would have slept forever if Mama hadn't woken me up the next morning. Then Reverend Parks bundled us all up in his wagon and carried us here to this big city. The biggest city in the world, I think it is, right on a huge big lake. He handed us over to a bunch of ladies from The Ladies Colored Fujitiv Association. I already knew how to spell Association. I'm still guessing at the word *Fujitiv.*

Next thing we knew, we were carried to a narrow brick house on a street full of houses and stores and more exciting things than I can begin to tell of. In a part of the city called St. John's Ward. Going to take me the rest of my life to write about what it's like here. A Mister Blunt owns the house and he's letting us board there. Mister Blunt says we can stay for as long as we need! He often rents to newcomers like us.

Says Papa and Mama and Thomas can get work and pay him when they do. Missus Blunt and Mama are getting on fine. They're two of a kind.

There's been no time for writing till now. Too many new things and too much happening! I'm almost getting used to it, but I still get scared now and then. We've been scared for so long, it's not something you get shut of easily. But the folks here are so kind. There are escaped slaves like us, then there's free colored folk like Reverend Parks who came up to Canada West from the states in the north. Seems like what we heard was true — they weren't safe there even though they were free. A man who went to Reverend Parks's church was snatched away from his family by a slave catcher in Ohio and sold down south even though he was a free man. Wasn't a thing he could do about it. Guess Papa was right when he said we should come up here.

I don't know what Mama would have done if they had taken my papa. I know she and Papa still mourn Caleb and Daniel and Sarah, but they never talk about it. If I mention their names, they just get all quiet and I know it hurts them, so I don't say anything more.

The colored folk hereabouts can do anything they

put a mind to. There's folk who own their own stores, even a doctor. The doctor lives right near to us.

And I've been going to school! Finally! Colored folk can get as much learning as they've a mind to in Canada. No laws against getting educated here. I do love that, but it's mighty strange sitting in a room with other children and all of us learning. And do you know the teacher's a white lady and us colored children are right in there with the white children. All of us learning together. I never would have believed it possible. Nobody's going to tell me I can't write, not ever again.

I never realized what being a slave really meant until now. I always just thought that was the way things had to be. Thought that whippings, and being hungry all the time, and being afraid of being sold away from our families was the way we were supposed to live. Now I know that's all one big lie. I wish I could tell everybody back home what living free is like. Wish they could live free, too. Only thing stops me from being so happy here is remembering them and knowing they're still living so hard. Young children like Bessie — all they got to look forward to for the rest of their lives is being slaves, and all they can hope for is not to be hurt too bad or sold away. I got a whole new life now. Makes me feel bad that

I am so blessed and they're not.

But right now I've got to stop. We're going to church and pray for Daniel and Caleb and Sarah, and for the end of the war, and after that Mama's going to Sabbath School. That's another school that the church runs after services, for grown-up folk who want to learn to read and write. The teacher there was carried up as a slave to Kingston — that's another big city here in Canada West — with a white family after the American War of Independence. Then she was freed by the Queen of England along with all the other slaves in Canada. Imagine that! Freed by a Queen! This surely is a special country. Teacher says some people here, like the ones she came up from the south with, are called Loyalists because they didn't want to be Americans — they stayed loyal to England. She asked Mama if she wanted to attend Sabbath School. I was surprised to hear Mama say that she did.

I think I'll tell Mama about my writing. I never would have thought it, but I suspect she'll approve.

Later

Showed Mama my writing. She was astounded. There's no other word for it. Said she couldn't believe

I'd been doing that all along. First off she started fussing at me for taking such a big chance while we were still slaves, and especially while we were running, but then she sort of ran her fingers over one of the pages and got all quiet.

"Read me a bit, Julia May," she said, so I read what I just wrote today. She reached over to give me a hug and I could see her eyes all shiny with tears.

I think she's proud of me.

Mama and Papa and Joseph and me are sharing a room almost as big as our whole cabin back on the plantation. Thomas is sleeping in the shed in the back yard. I'm so glad we got away before he was sold off. I never did get to know Caleb and Daniel too well, but Sarah was like a second Mama to me. I wonder where they all are now, but don't suppose I'll ever know for sure. Makes a big hurting sadness inside me that won't ever leave.

Mama and Papa have a big bed behind a curtain, but they're still downstairs talking to Missus Blunt. I'm curled up in the softest bed I've ever laid in. Joseph is snoring away beside me. He is snuffling in his sleep. I had to ask my teacher how to spell *snuffling*. Mama uses that word all the time. "Stop that snuffling and get to work now," she'll say. I always liked the sound of it but never knew what it would look like written down. I think it looks just as nice as it sounds — all those fat, round *ff*s. I most decidedly like writing letters with tails.

It's pretty cold here still, never mind that it is April. Be a lot warmer back in Virginia now. My old life there seems so far away! Does Miss Marissa wonder what happened to me? What would she think if she knew I was here in Canada? Free! I wonder if she would be happy for me. I bet her daddy isn't.

Monday, April 27*th*, 1863

Back to my own school today. My teacher's name is Miss Clarke. She's the nicest lady I ever met. I told her about my writing and she gave me a whole new scribbler just for me! She said writing things down that happen every day, like I've been doing, is called keeping a journal. So that's what I'm going to call my writing now. A journal. She even said when I use this notebook up she'll give me another one.

Miss Clarke is so quiet and gentle, not bossy at all. But the children are good as pie for her anyway. All but one boy who sits at the back. He acts up all the time. I think he can't learn anything and just wants to make sure nobody else has a chance to either. He made trouble all day until finally Miss Clarke had to take the strap to him. She didn't enjoy it the way our old overseer enjoyed whipping, though. She only gave him three licks, but Joey, he was hollering and crying fit to beat the band. Miss Clarke, she got tears in her own eyes and looked just as miserable as he did.

"Joey," she said, "This is hurting me as much as it hurts you. Please don't make me do it again."

And do you know, that boy sat still as a mouse for the rest of the day. Don't think he learned anything, though, and I expect he'll be up to his old tricks again tomorrow. Even when he's quiet, he's got the devil in his eyes.

Friday, May 1st, 1863

Mama got a job! Thomas and Papa haven't found anything yet, but they're looking. Missus Blunt and Mama have become real friendly, and Missus Blunt has a sister working at a big hotel down by the lake called The Queen's Hotel. Missus Blunt's sister was able to get Mama a job there taking in washing. She told the hotel people that Mama was an expert washerwoman who was used to doing laundry for fine folks.

Which is the truth, of course. Papa's been making the rounds of the stables, but nobody seems to need any more help, no matter how good he is with the horses. I know he's worried, but I'm praying he'll find something soon.

The Queen's Hotel where Mama's working is a place where people rent rooms and they get all taken care of. They're not letting Mama do the guests' washing yet, till they know for sure she's dependable. (Miss Clarke teaches us a new word every day and that's my word for today — *dependable*.) She's just doing some of the kitchen washing, tablecloths and all, but Mama's so good at everything she does, I reckon she'll be doing the guests' things soon.

Missus Blunt has a big washtub that she'll let Mama use out in the backyard. Mama will pay her out of her wages for the wood she uses to heat up the water. After school I go with Mama to collect the towels and sheets and stuff, then help her carry it home. Mama is not too happy about me even going near there — she says the hotel is full of soldiers and bad men and it's no place for a young girl. But Mama can't carry the washing all by herself, so she's made me promise to stay right close beside her.

The hotel is so big and so grand! There certainly

are a lot of rough looking men around, though, so I am careful to do exactly what Mama says.

It's worth your life to get across the street in front of the hotel, it's so wide and there are so many horses and wagons and buggies. The noise is enough to make a person deaf — everybody shouting and calling out, the horses whinnying and neighing. Those are two more new words I learned. Miss Clarke told me how to spell them. Don't they just sound like the noises the horses make? I told Joseph that and he went around whinnying and neighing and pretending he was a horse for the rest of the day until Mama put a stop to it.

Monday, May 4th, 1863

Mama and I go in the back door of the hotel. I stay in the kitchen with a girl name of Sibby while Mama collects the washing. Safe enough there. Sibby gave me a glass of water and told me stories about the people staying at the hotel. There are even Americans there! Officers' wives come up here to be safe from the war, she said. When she told me that I remembered that burned-out plantation we saw.

That started me to thinking. Escaped slaves like us

come up here to be free and away from our masters, then the masters come up here to be safe away from the war. Something wrong there.

Today she let me peek through the kitchen door into the dining room where everyone was eating their supper, but a little boy saw us and we had to duck back into the kitchen quick-like before he set up a scene.

Sibby's older than me, and colored like me, but she was born free here in Toronto. Her mama and papa came up from New York after the American Revolution. When Mama came to fetch me, Sibby said she'd look out for me tomorrow.

Imagine, a girl like me working and taking home wages every week!

Sunday, May 10ᵗʰ, 1863

Church today. We go to the British Methodist Episcopal Church. Miss Clarke helped me spell it. Sure is a long name. Good people there, though, and Reverend Brown preaches a fiery sermon. What I like best is the singing. There's lots of it. I haven't been singing much since Sarah was sold off, but I do enjoy the hymns and songs in this church. After services

Mama went to Sabbath School as usual, and I looked after Joseph. He was being a horse again today and it was really tiresome.

Thomas and Papa are still looking for jobs. No luck yet.

Monday, May 11th, 1863

Spelling is a mystery to me. Seems here in Canada they put *U*s in lots of words that they didn't in Virginia. Seems now I'm coloured with a *U*. Word looks a mite more elegant (that's my word for today), but it means the same. I want to please Miss Clarke so I'm trying my best to write proper and I'll put the *U*s in if I can figure out where they go.

Wednesday, May 13th, 1863

Rain today. Mama couldn't get the washing dry. It's hanging all over Missus Blunt's kitchen and she's none too happy about it.

Friday, May 15th, 1863

Something terrible happened today. I was walking down Queen Street with Joseph after school. Mama gave me a penny and I promised to buy him a candy from Missus Teakle's candy shop on Centre Street. That sure is a treat for him. For me, too. I like walking into a store and laying a penny on the counter and buying something. Never did that before in my life.

Anyway, we were walking home, and Joseph was too busy sucking on his candy to talk, which is unusual for him. He's so happy here, he's right back to being the rampageous (How's *that* for a word? I just made that up!) little boy he used to be. I was sort of daydreaming, I guess, and not paying much mind to what was going on or looking where I was going. All of a sudden I walked right into someone.

A man.

A white man.

He stumbled a bit, then reached out and grabbed my arm.

"Where do you think you're going, gal!" he shouted at me. He was holding my arm so tight it hurt. I got a big bruise there now.

I was so scared I couldn't say a word. I just stood there, staring at him. That made him even madder. He gave me a powerful shake, almost knocked me off my feet. Then Joseph shouted out for him to leave go of me and *kicked* him!

The man let me go and made a grab for Joseph, but Joseph is small and quick and he nearly got away, but the man caught him.

"Oh, no you don't!" the man cried. "You're going to pay for that, boy!" He raised his arm and was about to hit Joseph when another man on the street shouted at him.

"Leave that child alone!" he cried. He was a white man, too. Two more white men joined in, shouting at the man holding Joseph. Then a white woman strode right up to him and looked him square in the face.

"You leave that child alone," she yelled.

I never would have believed a white lady would do that. Especially to defend a coloured boy. The man let go of Joseph but he was still steaming mad. Then he took a good look at both of us.

"I know what these children are!" he said. "They're runaways for sure. I should take them back with me. Find their rightful owner."

Hearing that, I just turned cold from my head to my toes.

"Oh, no, you won't," one of the other men said. "They're free here. You can't touch them."

At that, Joseph lit out for home and I ran after him. We got back to Mister Blunt's and before I could warn Joseph not to say anything to Mama, he blurted the whole story out. That put Mama in a fury.

"I thought we were safe," she kept saying. "I thought we were safe!"

"We are," Papa told her. "Didn't those people protect Joseph? White people, they were."

That calmed her down a mite, but then Thomas started in to laughing. "Tell again about the lady yelling at the man," he said to Joseph.

That was all the encouragement Joseph needed. He told the whole story again and then he started laughing, too. Even Papa had to smile, but Mama didn't see one funny thing about it at all. She wouldn't let me go with her to take the washing back to the hotel and made me promise not to step foot outside Mister Blunt's house, or let Joseph out of my sight.

Monday, May 18th, 1863

A new boy came here yesterday. He escaped from Alabama, he said, and he'd been running for three months. Some folks carried him here and he's sharing the shed with Thomas. He's just about the same age as Thomas. I've never seen anyone so skinny and scared. Never seen anyone eat like he did tonight, either. Missus Blunt put a bowl of soup in front of him and he picked it up and slurped it so fast I was sure it was going to scald him all the way down. I thought Missus Blunt would be after him for bad manners, but she filled that bowl up again and watched him lap that down just as fast as the first one, then gave him a whole hunk of bread. That disappeared fast as the soup did. Guess he must've been half starved.

Made me remember what it was like when we were running. I almost forgot. Or maybe I just shut it up way back in my mind and I don't want to remember.

Wednesday, May 20th, 1863

Thomas is up to something, I know it. Something to do with that boy — Jeremiah, his name is. They were talking this morning in the kitchen before Thomas went out to work, but they stopped soon as I walked in. Thomas got a real guilty look on his face.

Thursday, May 21st, 1863

Miss Clarke says I'm learning so fast it plumb bedazzles her. Then she told me how to spell *bedazzle*. That's my favourite word yet. I never wrote *zz*s before. They're even more fun than *ff*s. They call the letter *z* "zed" here, not "zee" like back home. Can't for the life of me figure out why. Makes no sense at all.

Friday, May 22nd, 1863

Don't know what Thomas is up to, but he and that Jeremiah are planning something. Jeremiah's been resting up and eating all week and got his strength back by now. Papa asked him was he looking for work but he said he wasn't. Polite as he could be, but said he had other plans.

What other plans could a coloured boy have here? He's got to work!

Saturday, May 23rd, 1863

Well, we found out what plans that Jeremiah had, and they included Thomas. I can't set my mind straight, I am so shaken up. Don't know if I can even write of it.

This morning early, Thomas announced he had something to say. Jeremiah came into the kitchen but he stayed quiet by the door and let Thomas do the talking. Thomas said that Jeremiah told him that President Lincoln had created a regiment of coloured boys who could fight in the Union Army, and he and Jeremiah were going to go back south and sign up. I thought Papa would explode.

"Go *back!*" he shouted. "You crazy, boy? After all we've done to get up here safe, you're going to go *back?*"

Mama stared at Thomas and didn't say a word, but her whole face just kind of sagged. Joseph didn't rightly know what was going on but he knew it was bad and he ran to Mama and howled. I guess I just stood there with my mouth hanging open. For once I couldn't think of a thing to say.

Then it sank in. "You *can't!*" I just about screamed.

Thomas was looking all fierce but his mouth was set in that way that I know so well. Thomas sets his mouth like that, nothing's going to change his mind.

"I got a chance to fight, I'm going to do it," was all he said. "They beat us and sold us like animals. I want to pay them back."

"Thomas, think what you're doing!" Mama cried. I never heard so much pain in her voice. "I can't lose you, too!"

"Not going to lose me, Mama," he said. Tried to make his voice light, but it sort of broke halfway through. "I'll come back, I promise."

Then Papa turned to Jeremiah. He near roared at him. "This is your doing, boy! Why are you going back when you just got here and all these good folks have been helping you? Why are you taking my boy back with you?"

Jeremiah didn't answer for the longest time, then he sort of straightened up and looked Papa full in the face.

"My brother ran with me, sir," he said. "My baby brother. They shot him. Shot him in the back. He never had a chance. I'm going back to get revenge and stop them from ever doing that to anybody else again. Thomas — his brothers been sold off, even his sister. Maybe they're dead, too. He's coming with me because he wants to."

Then, I still can't believe it, Thomas picked up a bundle he had already packed, and he and Jeremiah made to go. Thomas tried to kiss Mama goodbye, but she just turned and ran out. He held out his hand to Papa and Papa took it. He hung onto it so long I thought he'd never let go and I swear I saw tears in his eyes. Papa. Who never cries.

"You keep that promise, hear?" was all he said, then he dropped Thomas's hand and followed Mama into the other room.

Joseph ran over to him and grabbed him around the knees. I just kept on standing there.

"Julia May?" Thomas said. "Aren't you going to wish me well?"

At that I just ran at him same as Joseph and glommed onto him just as hard. He gave me a hug that squeezed all the breath out of me, then bent and pried Joseph's fingers off. By then I was crying and Thomas was, too. I saw Jeremiah take off, then Thomas turned and followed him. I watched till they turned the corner of the street, and they were gone.

Mama took to her bed and Joseph and I did the washing, both of us crying hard. Papa sat with Mama for a spell, then took himself off to the stables.

Safe or not, seems like there's all kinds of ways to smash a family apart.

But Thomas isn't safe any more.

Monday, May 25th, 1863

Mama won't get out of bed. She won't even talk to me. I haven't seen her this upset since Sarah was sold off.

I stayed home from school today. Joseph and I did the washing for her. Joseph tried his best, but he's too small to be much help. It's heavy work. I told him he did good, though, and he managed a bit of a smile, then burst back into tears. I wanted to take the washing back to the hotel, but Missus Blunt wouldn't let me go on my own.

Tuesday, May 26ᵗʰ, 1863

Stayed home from school again today. Somebody's got to mind Joseph. They sent a boy around to find out why Mama hadn't taken the washing back. I promised we'd get it back tomorrow somehow. I'm afraid they'll let Mama go if we don't. Then what would we do?

Wednesday, May 27ᵗʰ, 1863

Papa carried the washing to the hotel today, and brought the dirty laundry back. Then he went into his and Mama's room and pulled the curtain closed behind him. He was in there a long time. I could hear his voice, talking low to Mama. Finally he came out, Mama behind him. She didn't say a word, but started in with the washing and shooed Joseph and me out. Joseph looked to be hurt and relieved all at the same time. I know just how he feels.

We were so happy there for a while. I keep telling myself that it will be all right. We're free, after all, and surely Thomas will come back to us when this war is over.

If he can.

~~If he doesn't get killed.~~

I'm not even going to think that.

Thursday, May 28th, 1863

I was so glad to get back to school today. Miss Clarke asked where I had been. I told a lie. Said I'd been sick. I can't bring myself to tell about Thomas yet. I feel like if I don't tell it out loud it won't be true. I'll walk in the house and there he'll be.

Papa's fretting a lot now. He's been able to find a bit of work now and then, mucking out stables here and there, but nothing permanent. And I guess he was hoping that Thomas would find work and be able to help out, too, but now he's gone we can't count on that. Mister Blunt says not to worry, we can stay here long as we want, but I know there's new people coming all the time and they need the room.

Sunday, May 31st, 1863

There was a new family in church today. But they won't be needing to stay at Mister Blunt's. They're free folks, came up from Ohio with a horse and a wagon just loaded with furniture and food. They're staying at a house just down the street from us. They got three sons, two older ones named Elisha and Jonah, and a boy just my age, name of Noah, but I don't like him much. He says I talk funny. Sounds to me like he's the one who talks funny. Talks like a Yankee.

Reverend Brown prayed for all the boys who had gone south to fight for the Union Army. Seems like Thomas and Jeremiah weren't the only ones. Mama started crying. Noah's mama put her arm around her. She's a nice lady, even if her Noah isn't. Her sons looked kind of shamefaced, I thought. Maybe they thought they should be going to fight, too.

Monday, June 1st, 1863

Wouldn't you know it, that Noah is coming to my school and he is even in the same classroom with me. He is a terrible show-off, but he can't write or read nearly as good as I can.

Tuesday, June 2ⁿᵈ, 1863

Had to stay home today. Joseph is sick.

Wednesday, June 3ʳᵈ, 1863

Home from school again. Joseph is worse. He has such a sore throat he cannot swallow anything. Mama tried to get him to gargle with muriatic acid and honey, but it just made him gag and vomit. It's really worrisome. Mama has to keep up with the washing for the hotel so I'm still staying home to care for him.

Thursday, June 4ᵗʰ, 1863

Noah's mama, Missus Long, came by today. She says we should call for Doctor Abbott who lives not too far from here in St. John's Ward. Mama's hesitant to do that, though. Even though he's a coloured man, he's a real doctor, graduated from university and all, and we don't have the money to pay him.

Friday, June 5ᵗʰ, 1863

Joseph's throat is a little better, but he's got a fever and a red rash all over him.

Saturday, June 6th, 1863

Joseph is so sick he's raving and seeing things that aren't there and talking all kinds of nonsense. He doesn't even know us! Missus Long is over here every day helping nurse him. She says lots of children are sick and Doctor Abbott is tending them. Mama finally gave in and Papa went for him. People got this sick back home, they usually died.

Later

Doctor came and went. Don't know if I feel better or not. He says Joseph's got something called Scarlet Fever. He got Mama to wring out a sheet in warm water, then wrapped Joseph all up in it and piled on every blanket we had in the house. Poor Joseph started in to sweating, but after a while he seemed a bit better and he's sleeping now. Doctor said when he wakes up tomorrow we have to give him eggnog and milk punch, and he left quinine and sweet spirits of nitre to dose him with four times a day. We have to give him a good purge, too, and keep sponging him off with hot water.

Missus Blunt's being good about letting us keep water boiling on her stove, but I've been set to keeping it supplied with wood.

Joseph is a little better. He's not seeing things anymore and he recognized Mama, even managed to sip a little bit of the eggnog that she made for him. It's got a little whiskey in it, Doctor said that would help bring his strength back. He's still got a fever, though, so we wrapped him up and got him to sweating again, then he went back to sleep.

Mama and Papa are off to church, but I'm staying with him. Makes my heart just feel like bursting to look at him sleeping there, he looks so small and helpless. We'll give him another sponge bath when they get back. I've got the water good and hot.

Monday, June 8th, 1863

Missus Long came over to watch Joseph so that I could go to school, but I no more than got there than my throat started in to hurt. I tried to pretend it didn't, then I vomited all over my desk. I don't know what was worse — how sick I felt or how humiliated. (That's another new word, but I'm not one bit happy to have to use it to describe what I went and did.)

Missus Long got me tucked up in bed alongside Joseph. Poor Mama. What's she going to say when she gets home and finds out she's got two sick children.

Missus Long just came in and gave me some honey and muriatic acid. Throat's hurting so much, but I managed to swallow it, then it came right back up.

My head is all swimmy and my eyes hurt. Can't write any more.

Monday, June 22nd, 1863

Today's the first day I can sit up and write, but my eyes still hurt and we've got to keep the room dark. Rash is gone, but I'm peeling and itching all over. Mama put lard all over me. That makes it even worse! Now I itch and I'm all greasy, too. I can't believe I've been sick for two weeks. Seems like I was in a dream.

Wednesday, June 24th, 1863

Still need the curtains closed over the window. Sunny today and the light hurts my eyes. I've been just as sick as Joseph, Mama says. I don't remember much about it. Mama says Missus Long is an angel. She's been taking care of me and also Joseph, who is feeling so much better he's running around now and vexing her something terrible. She scrubbed off the lard and rubbed me down with glycerine and rose water. That's a lot nicer. Feels cool and smells real good.

They couldn't get Doctor Abbott for me because he's gone off down south to be doctor to the Union Army, but Mama and Missus Long dosed me and wrapped me and sponged me just like they did for Joseph.

Papa's been cutting wood and carrying it home for Missus Blunt and he's been carrying the washing for Mama, too. He came in and sat by my bed today. Didn't say much, just held my hand, then gave me a kiss and a hug and went out. Joseph was acting up something terrible, but he just patted him on the head and didn't say anything, and his eyes got all teary. I guess he's glad he didn't lose his last two children.

Thursday, June 25th, 1863

I got up for a while today. My legs are weak as a newborn kitten's. Didn't help any that Joseph roared into the room and nearly knocked me down.

Saturday, June 27th, 1863

Thomas's birthday today. We none of us said a word, but I know we were all thinking about it.

Been a sad day.

Monday, June 29th, 1863

I'm finally well enough to go back to school. I'm so mad, though. I've missed so much and it will be over for the summer end of next month. I'm so mad! Just when I got the chance to really learn, I had to go and get sick. It's so unfair — Mama gets to keep on going to Sabbath School. It doesn't stop for the summer. She says I can go back in the autumn, but that's such a long time away. I'm going to keep on writing in my journal, though. That Noah came round and brought me all the lessons that I missed, so I'm going to work through them on my own. He had to brag about how much he learned while I was sick. Bet he still doesn't know as much as I do.

It was kind of him to bring me the lessons, though I expect his mama made him do it.

Tuesday, June 30th, 1863

Helped Mama carry the clean washing to the hotel today, but I couldn't carry much. Nearly all I could do just to walk there. I sat for a while in the kitchen, talking with Sibby while Mama collected the dirty laundry. We were peeking at all the fine people in the dining room. Sibby says more and more Americans from the

Confederate states are coming all the time. Guess that means the war isn't going so well for them. That's good news. Wonder if Thomas is fighting now? Wonder if he's killed anybody? That's a fearsome thought.

I won't let myself think any more thoughts like that.

Wednesday, July 1ˢᵗ, 1863

My hand is shaking so much I can hardly write.

When we were in the hotel today, Sibby and I peeked into the dining room, like we always do, and there, sitting right in front of my nose, were my old Missus and Miss Marissa!

I ducked back in like I'd been scalded. Sibby asked what was the matter, but I didn't dare tell her. Just said I was come over weak all of a sudden.

What if Missus Jackson saw me? What if she tries to get me back!

Rest of the time till Mama was ready to go I hid out in the kitchen. Wouldn't talk to Sibby, and all the way home with Mama, I had to bite my tongue. Wanted to tell her, but didn't dare. I knew how upset she'd be.

Don't know what to do!

Worse and worse!

I couldn't get up the nerve last night to tell Mama about seeing Miss Marissa and Missus Jackson, but I should have. Now we're all in a terrible way.

We were walking past the front door of the hotel this afternoon, like we always do on our way to the kitchen at the back, when at that very moment Miss Marissa and her mother walked out. Missus Jackson took one look at us and just shrieked. "That's my Selie!" she screamed, loud as could be. "That's my slave! She's a runaway!"

Everybody on the street stopped to look. Mama just froze right where she stood.

Then Miss Marissa saw me and she started in to screaming, too. "You ungrateful girl!" she shouted and started to run at me. "After I treated you so nice! Why did you run away?"

Then she came up so close I could feel spit flying from her mouth. "I'm going to see you get punished," she yelled. "I'm going to tell. I'm going to tell that you learned to read and write like the little sneak you are."

I didn't even stop to think, I was so stupefied. I just screamed right back at her. "I'm *allowed* here," I yelled. "I even go to school. I can read and write better than you!"

With that, Missus Jackson slapped me. Slapped me so hard I near fell down.

Well, that did it. Mama dropped the clean washing she was carrying, right there in the mud of the street. She stood herself in front of me and she faced Missus Jackson down.

"You can't hit my child here!" she cried. "We're in *Canada* now!" Then she grabbed my arm and pulled me away. We turned and raced back here as fast as we could. I collapsed on the front steps, but Mama just yanked me inside and slammed the door shut.

We've been waiting here for someone to come after us, but nothing's happened yet. I'm so scared I have to keep reminding myself to breathe.

Friday, July 3rd, 1863

No one came, but Mama won't let me out of her sight. She even kept me home from school. We haven't heard a thing from Missus Jackson, but the hotel sent a boy round to say Mama was let go on account of her dropping all the washing in the mud. We're still nervous as cats, but I guess it's true that

Missus Jackson can't get at us here in Canada. Besides, Papa says if she's in Canada, it must mean she's not safe in Virginia, and she's not about to return or try to carry us back.

I guess I know now how Miss Marissa feels about me running off. She's not happy for me, that's for certain. I should have known it. Should have expected it, but I didn't. We used to play together when we were little, and I thought we were almost friends, even though she was my mistress, but I was wrong. I was just her slave, after all. She never cared a bit for me.

Plain stupid of me to feel so bad about it.

Mama and Papa are arguing something fierce. Mama wants to leave right away. But where could we go?

Saturday, July 4th, 1863

Missus Long has been here talking to Mama all day. She says they're all going to leave Toronto and go farther north to some place near a village called Durham. Says they're farmers and they've given Toronto a try but they really don't like city living. No jobs here for Mister Long or the boys. I think maybe she's scared, too, that her boys might up and go join the

Union Army like Thomas did if they can't get any work here. She's got a sister living near Durham with her family, and that sister's been writing Missus Long letter after letter begging her to come up to them. Missus Long says there's land to be had for coloured folk up there and we should go with them. Her sister's well fixed and can help out any way we need till we get settled in proper. Papa's home now and Mister Long's talking with him.

Imagine having kinfolk! I haven't any kin that I know of except my own family, and most of them are gone. Mama was sold off when she was pretty young, but she remembers her mama and her two sisters. No way of knowing whatever happened to them. Papa says he must have been sold off when he was a bit younger than Joseph, because he can barely remember his mama, but not his papa. Says he remembers he might have had a big brother, but he can't recollect for sure. No telling what their names were.

It's like I have this big, unknown family of ghosts. But imagine having a real aunt or an uncle! And cousins! I used to call folks Aunt or Uncle back on the plantation, but they weren't really kin. It was just more polite that way. And Missus Long says her papa lives with her sister and her family, too. Imagine having a grampa! Noah sure is lucky.

But I don't want to leave Toronto. I want to keep on going to school. I like it here better than any place I've ever been. I may not have kinfolk but I'm beginning to have friends. I don't want to start running again.

Sunday, July 5th, 1863

We're going whether I like it or not. After church Mama and Papa sat down with Joseph and me and told us. We're leaving next week. Mama's too afraid to stay in the same city as Missus Jackson. Papa's discouraged about not finding work, too. Figures he might do better if we go up north with Mister and Missus Long.

Moving again!

I hate this!

I hate Missus Jackson!

I hate Miss Marissa!

Why did they ever have to come to Toronto? Haven't they done hurt enough to us?

Tuesday, July 7th, 1863

I've been too angry to write, but we're leaving tomorrow and I don't know when I'll get another chance. The most amazing thing happened today. Mama didn't let me go back to school, but Miss Clarke came by here. She said she heard we were leaving and she wanted to say goodbye. Told me again what a smart girl I was. Said I should keep on with my schooling no matter what. Then — I near dropped dead with surprise — she put her arms around me and gave me a hug. I couldn't help it, I started in to crying. She gave me another hug and then she left.

Now I got to pack up my things. I don't have much, but I'm going to take my journal and all my school work. Mama says it will be different from before. We're not running and we'll have the wagon to ride in and carry our possessions in. She says we should thank the Lord for the kindness of the Longs.

I do thank Him. But I still do not want to go.

Wednesday, July 8th, 1863

It is different this time. First of all, we're travelling right out in the open in the daytime. No hiding, no running. No dogs chasing after us. It was a bright, sunny day, not too hot, and if I weren't so riled up about Marissa and having to leave Toronto, I might even have enjoyed it, but for one thing. Except for Mister Long driving, only Joseph was riding in the wagon. I was determined to walk just like Noah, but along about noon time I got so tired I couldn't anymore. Mister Long saw me lagging and just lifted me up and plopped me in the wagon before I could protest. Guess I'm still weak from being so sick, but I'm going to walk farther tomorrow, and farther than that the day after. Noah, of course, just swaggered on with Elisha and Jonah and acted all superior.

We left Toronto by way of Yonge Street. It wasn't too bad at first, but soon got muddy. That's one reason why I got so tired. Pretty hard slogging through all that mud. The sun dried it up a bit, though, and the going got easier.

Joseph is in his element, as Miss Clarke used to say. He is so crazy mad about horses. He persuaded Mister Long to let him sit up on the seat beside him and hold the reins. Then, when we stopped here in the woods where there's a little stream to provide us with water, Mister Long let him fill the feedbag and helped him put it on the horse. The horse's name is Luck. Joseph is standing up on a stump and currying and brushing it to death right now. He's singing a little song to it! Made up words, all about a big strong hero of a horse. Most foolish thing I ever heard. Horse seems to like it, though. Keeps twitching one ear after the other as if he's listening.

Elisha shot a squirrel and Missus Long and Mama have squirrel stew boiling away over the fire. Smells good. Joseph trails after Elisha and Jonah all the time. I guess he misses Thomas. They're nice boys, though, and they don't seem to mind. They're lots nicer than Noah.

It does make the dark seem less fearful when you can have a fire! And when you got lots to eat.

The Longs have two old army tents to sleep in tonight, but we're going to put blankets down beside the wagon and prop a tarp over us. Lucky it's not raining, but the mosquitoes are fierce! I'm bit to pieces.

Papa's being awful quiet. I think he's feeling as bad as I am about leaving Toronto. If he'd been able to get a job, maybe we might have been able to persuade Mama to stay.

But probably not. Not with Missus Jackson there and Mama losing *her* job and all.

I sure hope things get better for us, wherever we're going.

Thursday, July 9th, 1863

Went through a town called Richmond Hill today. The Longs tried to stay at a tavern tonight, but the owner just chased them away really rudely. Said they didn't cater to coloured folk. We may be free in Canada, but it seems we're not always welcome. It was different in Toronto, we kept to our own neighbourhood for the most part, but out here there's mostly white people and they're not all friendly.

Friday, July 10th, 1863

Turned west today. At first it was real pleasant. Lots of little farms and villages along the way, but then it started to rain. Turned the road back into a muddy, squishy mess. In places it was so swampy there were logs put crosswise, side by side, to make a kind of trail through the trees and bushes to walk on. Poor Luck had a hard time of it. His hooves kept slipping and sliding on the logs. Mister Long walked up beside him, leading him by the halter, and the boys pushed the wagon from behind. Joseph, of course, had to push, too, even though he was more of a nuisance than a help, I reckon. Mama was afraid he would fall, and fall he did. By the time we stopped here tonight he was mud from head to toe. No way to wash him up, though, so he's just huddled here beside me, wet and smelly.

We couldn't make a fire, just ate some bread and cold leftover squirrel stew. It wasn't nearly as good as it was last night.

I wasn't too unhappy about riding in the wagon today, even though Noah pranced around pretending not to mind the rain. He's just as muddy and wet as Joseph now, though, and I suspect he's just as miserable as the rest of us.

Saturday, July 11ᵗʰ, 1863

No rain today, the Lord be thanked. We got to a little village called Bolton. There's a tavern here but they're making us stay in the stable. No coloured people allowed in that tavern, either. Actually, I'm just as glad. The tavern's no more than a log shanty and when I peeked in I've never seen any place so dirty and stinky. The stable is much nicer and the horses smell nicer, too.

Good chance to dry out and wash up at the pump in the yard. Luck seems happy to be in a warm dry place with other horses. He keeps making funny little nickering noises and they make noises right back at him. Joseph says they're talking to each other. I could almost believe him.

Papa told me a bit more about where we're going. Missus Long's sister and her family live on a farm near the village of Durham in a place called the Queen's Bush. Guess it belongs to that same Queen who made all the slaves in Canada West free. Missus Long says they're going to get a piece of land, too, and set up farming there. I asked Mama if we were going to farm, but she didn't answer me. The Longs had a farm in Ohio so they know all about that, but my Papa doesn't know anything but tobacco planting and tending horses, and Mama has always worked in the Big House. Besides, without Thomas, there would be too much work for Papa to do on a farm.

I wonder if Thomas would've left if he had known we'd be moving on from Toronto? Mama worries that he won't be able to find us, but Reverend Brown said as long as we keep in touch with him, he'll let Thomas know where we are when he gets back.

And he will get back.

He will.

We made a fire and had soup tonight. The cook at the tavern was more friendly than the owner, and he gave Mama a good bone with lots of meat left on it, and a loaf of bread. The bread was hard as a rock, but tasted fine when I dunked it in the soup to soften it up. My stomach is a lot happier now. I felt so good that before I started to write in this journal, I dug down into my pack and got out my school work. I've been reading it over and remembering what Miss Clarke told me.

Something real strange happened. Noah came over and sat down beside me. I got all fussed and started to shove my stuff back in my pack, but he stopped me.

"Can I read, too?" he asked.

Could have knocked me over with a feather. Before I could answer he went on, saying that he hadn't brought any workbooks with him and he'd be pleased if I'd let him look at mine. Said it all in such a nice, polite way that I couldn't say no. So we sat there and went over lessons together.

Who would have believed it?

Sunday, July 12th, 1863

There's a little church here where we attended services this morning before setting out. We were all a little shy because there were only white folks there, but we figured they couldn't throw us out of a *church*, so we just stood real quiet-like in the back by the door. At first nobody seemed to mind. The Reverend preached a powerful sermon all about hellfire. I didn't understand most of it, but it sounded fine. Except I did see one man nodding off until his wife gave him a poke that woke him up with a jump. Then she saw us and she gave us a good glare. Guess she didn't like coloured folk being there but, hey, *we* were awake.

Sunny, hot and even more mosquitoes today. I itch all over. Scratched both legs raw.

More farms around here. Farmer let us stay in his barn tonight. Very different from hiding in barns on the Underground Railroad, though. One thing, we're staying at night and can sleep easy. Other thing, we can make a fire and use the pump in the stable yard for water. And I don't have to hide that I'm writing in my journal. I read to Mama from it all the time now. She enjoys that and it helps her learn, too. She liked going to the Sabbath School in Toronto and I think she misses it.

Safe or not, I couldn't settle down last night. Kept waking up and hearing strange noises. It was so dark in that barn. Kept thinking I heard dogs. Then a dog did howl and I was so scared I almost screamed right out loud. Mama and Papa sat bolt upright when they heard it, then Joseph started in to crying. We all huddled together and couldn't sleep the whole rest of the night.

We knew we were safe. Knew it was just the farmer's dog. But knowing that is one thing, and remembering the terrible time when we were running is another.

The Longs didn't even wake up. They may be coloured like us, but they've never been slaves, and they never had to run like we did.

The road we're on is called the Toronto-Sydenham Road. Missus Long was telling Noah and me. We're going up it till we get to the Durham Road, then turn off on it. Her sister's farm is about half a day's travel from there. Be about another week from here, she reckons. We got through the swamp all right and the road is a lot better. Even got gravel on it. Joseph says Luck is much happier. I'll take his word for it as I don't seem to have his talent for talking to horses.

Tuesday, July 14th, 1863

Passed through a village called Mono Mills. They let us stay in the stables of a hotel there. Joseph is brushing Luck. I swear, he's going to brush that horse bald.

Noah got a heel of bread and some cheese from a girl in the kitchen and brought it out to me. We sat and went through our lessons as usual. I kind of like that now, and look forward to it.

Can I possibly be beginning to like Noah?????

Thursday, July 16th, 1863

Hot today. Almost as hot as summer back in Virginia. We're in a place they call Jelly's Corners today. It's not really a village. Just a few cabins and a tavern owned by Mister Jelly. We didn't even bother asking if we could stay there. Besides, it was pretty small and rough looking. We're staying in a farmer's field near a little creek. That cool water did taste good when we finally got here.

Friday, July 17th, 1863

Heard wolves howling last night, and this morning when I went out to relieve myself in the bushes I saw wolf tracks in the mud around the stream where we fetched our water. I got myself back to our camp real fast, I can tell you. Gives me a real spooked feeling to think wolves are prowling around so near to us while we sleep. I kept imagining I saw a wolf behind every tree all the rest of the day.

Saturday, July 18ᵗʰ, 1863

Flesher's Corners today. A real village with a post office called the Artemesia Post Office, because we're in the Township of Artemesia. Mister Long told me that. Best of all, it's at the corner of the Toronto-Sydenham Road and the Durham Road. Tomorrow we'll be at Missus Long's sister's farm! Missus Long is so excited, she can't stop talking. She's been telling Mama over and over all about her sister, and her sister's husband, and all her sister's children. She's got about six. The more she talked, the quieter Mama got. I knew Mama was thinking about Sarah and Daniel and Caleb. And Thomas, of course. And probably about her lost sisters, too. Being Mama, she just nodded, polite as could be, and didn't let on that anything was wrong, but I could tell she was hurting. I slipped over beside her and took her hand. She gave mine a good squeeze and I know it comforted her a little bit.

Monday, July 20th*, 1863*

Couldn't write yesterday, too much confusion. We passed through three little villages on the Durham Road — one of them called Virginia, imagine that! — and got to Missus Long's sister's farm late in the afternoon. Missus Thornton, her name is. When we drove up, it seemed like the cabin just exploded, with children all running out to greet us. Missus Thornton stood behind them in the doorway, holding her hands so tight together it seemed like she was afraid they would fly away. Missus Long ran to meet her. Missus Thornton let loose her hands and ran to meet Missus Long with her arms outstretched wide and they met halfway. They just stood there hugging, and paying no mind at all to the commotion going on around them. Don't think they even noticed it.

The children — there seemed to be at least twenty of them — circled the wagon and clamoured at us. One who looked to be about Joseph's age climbed up the wheel and grabbed the reins from Joseph before anyone could stop him. Of course Joseph wasn't having one bit of that, so he hit the boy and the boy hit back, and next we knew they had fallen off the wagon and were fighting in the dirt.

What an arrival that was!

Tuesday, July 21st, 1863

I've got the family sorted out now. There are only six children after all, although the smaller ones are so wild it just seems like more. The youngest is the boy, Nat, who fought with Joseph yesterday. They're still fighting. Then there are three girls, the oldest just about my age, and two older brothers about the same age as Elisha and Jonah. The girl my age's name is Adaline. She seems friendly, but she's very quiet. Not surprising. Everyone else in the family makes so much noise. Missus Thornton is just as nice as Missus Long. She's a bit older, I think. Mister Thornton is as quiet as Adaline. I think he lets his wife and his children do all the talking, and they certainly do a good job of it. There's no boy Noah's age so I think he's feeling a bit left out.

The Longs are staying in their tents and we're in the barn with Luck and an ox and a cow. Very warm and friendly in here. I'm a bit shy about writing in front of all the others, so I'm doing it here, out of sight.

Oh, drat. Here come Joseph and Nat. The two of them are actually walking together, but pummelling each other as they go along. I'll put this away for now.

I'm wondering what we are going to do. The grown-ups stayed up late last night, talking serious. They're not looking too happy today.

Wednesday, July 22ⁿᵈ, 1863

Well, now I know. We're not staying and neither are the Longs. There's no land to be had anymore. When the Thorntons came there was lots of land available, and coloured people were welcome to settle on it. So many more white people are moving up here now, though, that they're taking the land back. The Thorntons had cleared a few acres just behind their farm, and that's what they were going to give to Mister and Missus Long, but they lost them to a white family just two weeks ago. There was nothing they could do about it, and there wasn't time to tell Mister and Missus Long before they set out from Toronto. Missus Long is looking pretty sad. I guess she was really looking forward to living near her family.

Seems there is land just a bit farther north though, around a place called Owen Sound, and that's where we're going. The Longs will be able to farm, and Mister Thornton says the town of Owen Sound is big enough that we'll be able to live there and maybe Mama and Papa will be able to find work. I hope so. I can't bear how worried they both look.

I'm sorry for Mister and Missus Long, but I'm glad that we're not staying here. I liked living in Toronto and I'd much rather live in a town than on a farm and I'm sure Mama and Papa feel the same way. I'm sorry to leave Adaline, though. She might have been a friend.

Mister Long and Elisha and Jonah have the wagon all ready. We're off! I think the Longs would have liked to stay and visit more, but I can tell they're worried now and want to get somewhere where they can settle down as soon as they can. They don't want to take a chance that the land in Owen Sound will be all gone before they get there, too.

Thursday, July 23rd, 1863

We passed through the village of Durham today. Now we're on the Garafraxa Road to Owen Sound. I really really like that name — Garafraxa. Rough road, though, in spite of its pretty name. I was getting jounced around so much in the wagon that I got off and walked. I'm much stronger now.

Saturday, July 25th, 1863

Through Chatsworth today. The Garafraxa Road meets up here with the road we were on before, the Toronto-Sydenham Road, and we're following that to Owen Sound.

Sunday, July 26th, 1863

We're here! Late this afternoon we came to the top of a hill and below us we saw the town all spread out around a harbour full of steamers and sailing vessels, with a river running down to it through the town.

Missus Long's sister gave us directions to a house in Owen Sound called Sheldon Place, so that's where we headed. It's on another hill on the other side of town from where we came in. Owen Sound just hunkers down in between those two hills at the mouth of that river that flows out to Georgian Bay and Lake Huron.

Sheldon Place is owned by a white man, Mister Frost, and Missus Long said she'd heard tell that he's built cabins on his property for escaped slaves just like us. We asked directions from a coloured man on the main street, but when we found it, we could hardly believe it. Sheldon Place is almost as big as the Big House at our old plantation. Mister Long turned the wagon in through the gate, but we didn't dare pull up to the front door. While we sat there in the wagon, just sort of staring at the house, the door opened and a girl came out. I thought she'd scold us for being so uppity, she being white, but she just greeted us as nicely as you could want and said she'd go fetch Mister Frost. A tall white man came out. He looked kind of stern, but he was followed by a lovely white lady with silver hair and the sweetest smile on her face. He walked over to us and shook Mister Long's hand, and then held out his hand to Papa. "I'm John Frost," he said, "and this is Missus Frost. You're welcome here."

Just like that! The girl showed us to a cabin and told us it was ours for as long as we needed it. Mister Frost is going to help the Longs find a piece of land to farm somewhere around here, too. In the meantime, they're staying in a cabin right next to us. We have our whole cabin to ourselves! It's got a kitchen with a wood stove and a table with benches on either side of it. Even got a sideboard to put dishes on, not that we have any dishes, but I reckon we'll get some. Then there's another room for Mama and Papa, with a bed with a feather tick on it, and another little room where Joseph and I will sleep. Two little cots in there for us, with quilts on them. The Longs' cabin is just about the same, but they don't plan on staying there for long.

Hmm. Think I just made a joke there and I didn't even mean to.

We weren't hardly settled in when two men came over to help Mister Long unload the wagon, and two ladies took Mama and Missus Long in hand. A passel of children came running to check us out and Joseph found a kindred spirit right away — Mama's going to have trouble there — but I didn't see any other girls my age.

It's like a whole little community — all the people are slaves who escaped and made their way up here, just like we did. Feels so comfortable and safe. I don't think I feel so bad about leaving Toronto now.

We didn't get to church today, but it's the Sabbath, and Mama wanted to make our own little service right here. We had supper with the Longs, then we came back and gathered together in the kitchen.

Mama told us to hold hands, so we made a circle, Mama, Papa, Joseph and me, and Papa prayed. First of all he gave thanks that we've found such a secure haven after all our journeys, then he prayed for Thomas's safety. Then he prayed for Caleb and Daniel and Sarah, that they be under our dear Lord's wing wherever they are. Happy though I am, I couldn't help crying a bit. Mama was crying too, though, and I even saw Papa swipe at his eyes when he didn't think anyone was looking.

Monday, July 27th, 1863

It's very late, but I want to write this down. An old man came by this evening and sat for a while in front of one of the cabins. The people here all seem to know him. Old Man Henson, they call him. Noah ran to get me because he said the old man was telling stories about his life and it was real interesting. When I followed Noah over to where he was, most all of the people in the community had gathered round to listen to him.

He said his mother's mother was the daughter of an African chief before she was stolen away and sold into slavery in America. He grew up on a plantation in Maryland and married another slave named Emily. Even though he's old, his voice got all soft when he talked about her. Somebody asked him where she was but then he got mournful. When he ran away she wouldn't go with him. Maybe she was too afraid. He's never seen her since. I think that's the saddest thing. Then he started to sing and some of the others joined in. I couldn't help humming along a bit, quiet-like. I love singing so much. A lady near me said, "Sing up, girl. You've got a right pretty voice!" But it made me so shy I just snuck away back here. I can hear them singing still, their voices coming tranquil through the dark. I'm sitting outside on the stoop of the cabin all by myself. Mama and Papa have gone to listen to the old man, and Joseph is asleep.

Not quite all by myself. A mangy old dog has just come and settled down beside me.

Tuesday, July 28ᵗʰ, 1863

There's going to be a picnic just for us coloured folk on Saturday to celebrate Emancipation Day. That's the day slavery ended here in Canada, thirty years ago. Coloured folk have been free here for thirty years! The picnic's going to be at a place called

Presque Isle up the shore a ways from here. That's French for "almost an island." One of our neighbours told me that when I asked. Told me how to spell it, too. Reason it's called that is because it's a piece of land that sticks out into the Bay and it's almost cut off into an island. Imagine — I know words in French!

Folks are going on a steamer. There'll be speeches and games and all sorts of fun. The Longs are going and Noah can't stop talking about it.

Wish I could go, too, but it costs money.

Wednesday, July 29th, 1863

I'm going! Missus Long invited me. At first Mama got all stiff because she didn't want the Longs to pay for me, but Missus Long said that with nothing but useless boys around her, she needed someone to help her fix their picnic hamper, and help her at the picnic, and if I did that, I would earn my way. She said she missed having a girl around and she'd take it kindly if Mama would lend me to her. It took a lot of persuading, but Mama and Missus Long are such good friends, Mama finally gave in.

I will be the best helper Missus Long ever had. I can't wait!

That dog's still following me around. He's not mangy and he's not that old.

Thursday, July 30th, 1863

Gave the dog a bath. He's really not a bad-looking dog. Sort of brown and scruffy. Calling him Boze. Don't know where I got that name from, but it suits him.

Friday, July 31st, 1863

The picnic's tomorrow! I've been helping Missus Long get food ready every minute of my spare time. We are going to eat well. Fried chicken, ham salad, greens and berry pie for dessert. Mama made some of her good Virginia cornbread for us to take, too.

Saturday, August 1st, 1863

I think I had more plain and simple fun today than I've ever had in my life. We were afraid it was going to rain, but the sun came out just as I was leaving to go over to the Longs' cabin. Noah and his brothers toted the hamper and we all made our way down to where the steamer was waiting in the harbour. The

Alderson, it was called. There was a big crowd all around, waiting to get on it, and everybody was as excited as I was. Finally, the steamer gave a big blast with its whistle, and a gangplank was lowered to the shore for us to get on. We were almost the first people on! We went up to the top deck and found a spot for ourselves right at the front. (The "bow" it's called on a boat — Noah told me that.) We wanted to be able to see everything. The sun was full out by then and it was a fine day.

I couldn't help remembering the last time I was on a steamer. It was so different today. We were all so tired, and hungry and plain scared back then. Didn't know what was going to happen to us. Couldn't have imagined how good it was all going to turn out. I remembered standing in the wind on that boat and saying to myself that it was the wind of freedom that was blowing in my face. The wind was blowing today, too, and I just drank it in and said a quiet little prayer of thanks to the Lord for bringing us safely through such trouble. Added on a bit for Thomas and Caleb and Daniel and Sarah. I can't ever be thankful for my good fortune without remembering them.

It took us almost an hour to get to Presque Isle. We got off there and found a place to lay down our blanket and set up our picnic. The shore is all stony, but it's really pretty around here. The water is so clear you can see fish swimming around in it. At least you could at first. Some boys set to hurling stones at them the minute they got there, and the fish cleared out pretty quick after that.

Too bad Joseph isn't here. He'd have loved to join in. Actually, it's just as well he isn't here. The engine room on the boat was completely open. I looked in when we were getting off. It was all hot and noisy, with big machines pounding away and a sailor loading wood into the furnace. If Joseph had been around he'd have been in there and into some kind of trouble for sure.

At first the children in the group just ran around exploring. Noah and his brothers and his papa had brought fishing lines and went out on the point to see if they could catch anything, but they didn't. Guess those fish knew well enough to keep far away today. I helped Missus Long set out our picnic, then we called them to come eat. We had a feast.

After people had eaten their lunches and settled down, we had speeches. Lots of speeches. I got to admit that I didn't listen too hard, but the grown-up people liked them. There was lots of clapping and encouragement. Old Man Henson was there and he spoke about his early days. Lady sitting next to us told us he's about a hundred years old but I think she might have been exaggerating. He is pretty old, though.

What with the sun so hot, and all that good food, I just lay down on my back and watched the clouds go by. Almost went to sleep. I only perked up when the singing started. Then there were games for the children, and the grown-ups visited back and forth.

It was late afternoon by the time we got back on the boat and headed home. The sun was setting over the shore and I stood at the rail and drank it all in. When we reached the cabin it was dark. I helped Missus Long unpack their hamper and tidy things up, then came on here to home.

I still got the sound of singing in my head, and a warm, happy feeling inside of me.

Sunday, August 2nd, 1863

Went to the British Methodist Episcopal Church. The preacher today was Father Miller. He's a kindly man. Talked about following the teachings of Jesus Christ, and the Paradise that awaits us if we do. Made it sound pretty nice. I wanted to ask if people up there are black and white, like down here, or if our souls are all the same colour, but Mama shushed me.

Monday, August 3rd, 1863

Made a friend today, and she's a white girl! Name of Amelia. I hope she turns out nicer than Miss Marissa. I think she will, though, on account of she doesn't own me. This is how it happened.

There's a kind of woods behind our cabins, and a big sort of cliff behind them. The West Rocks, one of the children here said it was called. Said it was a great place to explore and climb, but his mama didn't let him because she thought it was too dangerous. That got me curious, of course, so I decided I would just go and have a look-see. It was pretty hard going getting through the bush (that's what they call woods here) and about halfway there I stumbled into a wet, boggy patch and sank in nearly up to my ankles. Horrible black, smelly stuff it was. I knew Mama was not going to be one bit happy when she saw the state of my boots when I got home. Anyway, I got past that part and came up against the cliff. I wasn't really intending to go up it, but I thought I'd just climb a bit. Boze was with me, but I made him stay at the bottom. The rocks there are all jumbled up and slippery with moss. Not too hard climbing for me, but not good for a dog. Boze wasn't too happy about it, but he did what I told him. Seems like a good dog. I never had a dog before. Dogs were just animals to be scared of, but I kind of like having Boze around. He's good company.

I meant to stop, but somehow just kept on going. There's cracks in between the rocks where a body could fall, so I guess that's why that boy's mama didn't want him fooling around in there, but I'm pretty spry and it didn't seem dangerous to me. Before I knew it, I'd climbed almost all the way to the top. Then stones started rattling down on top of me. I realized there was somebody else up there. I froze still as I could, and I got to admit my heart was beating pretty hard. No telling who was there and I was all by myself. Then I heard a slipping and sliding kind of noise and next thing I knew a girl landed down beside me with a thump. She didn't see me at first and let loose with the kind of cuss word that would get me a slap from Mama if she heard it. Then she got up and saw me there. For a moment we just looked at each other and neither one of us said a word.

"Who are you," she asked, "and what are you doing here?"

Well, the way she said it just got my back up.

"I'm Julia May Jackson," I said right back at her, as prideful as I could, "and I wasn't aware this was private property." I was all of a sudden mad and ready to light right into her, but she just shook her hair out of her eyes and grinned at me.

"Sorry," she said. "You just surprised me. I didn't know anybody else was here. Not too many children are allowed."

"I'm allowed," I said, although that wasn't the exact truth. Mama didn't tell me not to climb up here, but that's only because she didn't know about it.

"My name's Amelia," she said then. "Pleased to meet you."

Took all the wind out of my sails, the friendly way she said it.

"Come on," she said, "I'll show you an easy way down."

We climbed down together. She showed me how to avoid the boggy bit and we got back out of the bush. Turns out she lives up near Mister Frost's place. Her daddy's a ship's captain on one of the steamers I saw in the harbour on Saturday. She had to hurry home on account of it was suppertime by then, but she said she'd meet me there again tomorrow and show me all around. Show me the best climbing places, and even some caves.

Mama did light into me about the state my boots were in, and the state I was in, too, but I didn't mind. I'm too busy thinking about tomorrow. Boze was about as dirty as he was when I first found him, so he got another bath. So did I.

Tuesday, August 4th, 1863

Amelia's mother is the nicest lady. I met Amelia again today and we spent the whole afternoon exploring and climbing around the rocks. Then Amelia asked me if I wanted to go home with her. I wasn't too sure that I should — we were both pretty dirty — but she told me her mother wouldn't care, and she didn't. She just took one look at us and sent us to the pump out back to wash up, then when we came back she had glasses of fresh, cool milk sitting on the kitchen table for us, and the most delicious molasses cookies. Amelia has little twin sisters, Nell and Mary, and they sat with us and stared at me, but I didn't mind.

Amelia's mother asked me all sorts of questions about where we came from and how we made it up here. She kept saying, "My, my, what a story!" I got carried away and talked more than I have to anybody about what it was like. She made Boze stay outside, but Mama does that too so I didn't mind. Boze might have, though. I snuck a morsel of cookie out to him when I went home.

Tomorrow Amelia's daddy, Captain Pearce, is sailing off to Collingwood and Amelia invited me to go down with her to wave him off. She has a brother, too, named William, and he's going to be a sailor when he's old enough. He doesn't pay Amelia and me much attention — thinks he's too grand for consorting with his sister and her little friends, I guess.

Wednesday, August 5ᵗʰ, 1863

Papa got a job in a stable here! He's been helping out with Mister Frost's horses and I guess Mister Frost was pretty impressed with how good Papa is with them, because he put in a good word for Papa with a friend of his, Mister Cooper, who owns a stable in Owen Sound, and Mister Cooper hired him. We are all so happy about that. Papa's mighty pleased, too, I can tell. And relieved. Mister Long told us that the white people in Owen Sound are beginning to resent coloured people taking their jobs, so it's getting harder and harder for our men to find jobs here. He's all for Papa going into farming like they're going to do, but Papa doesn't want to do that. Mama doesn't either. Thank goodness.

Joseph, of course, is delighted that Papa will be working with horses and he pestered and pestered until Papa agreed to carry him to work with him. Joseph is determined to help but I think he'll be more of a hindrance than anything else.

We went down to see Captain Pearce's steamer off. What a commotion! It went off in a bluster of whistles and black smoke, the engines just churning up the water in the harbour. It's a much bigger boat than the steamer we went down to Presque Isle on. Amelia says her mother worries about her daddy — there've been a lot of shipwrecks in the lake here. Glad Mama didn't know that before I went on the picnic.

Thursday, August 6th, 1863

Missus Frost has given Mama washing to do. She asked if Mama could iron and Mama said she certainly could, so Missus Frost said she could find lots of work for her, and she's going to give her ironing to do, too. Mama can work right up at Sheldon Place with the white girl they got helping out as a servant there.

Thank goodness again for the kindness of Mister and Missus Frost. We are certainly grateful to them. We can start to be independent now with Mama and Papa both working, and that's a good feeling for all of us.

Saturday, August 8th, 1863

Joseph is a trial. He has decided to be a horse again and there's no talking to him. He scurries around on all fours, neighing and whinnying and kicking his heels up. Mama got so provoked with him that she put his dinner on the floor and told him if he was going to be an animal, he could eat like an animal. Didn't seem to bother Joseph none, but then Boze started inching in, his eye on a chicken bone, and Joseph decided to leave off being a horse long enough to eat at the table.

Papa just laughs.

Sunday, August 9th, 1863

Church again today. I am getting very fond of Father Miller. Couldn't meet with Amelia, though, as she goes to the white folks' church and Mama won't let us do a thing on the Sabbath but sit around home. Only good thing is that I don't even have to do chores. We're putting in a little vegetable patch, even though it's so late in the season, and I'm tired of digging. The soil here is too hard and stony. Won't have much time before winter sets in, but Mama says we might get some radishes and young carrots, and the ground will be ready for planting then come spring.

Monday, August 10th, 1863

There are Indians around town here. Some of them carry people across the river in their canoes, but they don't live here anymore. Amelia says they used to, but they've been moved up the peninsula to Cape Croker. She says they like it there, but I wonder. If they were here first, I don't see how they would take kindly to being moved out.

Anyway, we saw an Indian lady on the street today and Amelia said she had her land taken away and she was fighting for it. Amelia said she went all the way to England to see the Queen and tell her about it, but it doesn't seem to have done her much good. I could hardly believe it, but Amelia swears it's true. She's got an Indian name which I cannot begin to spell, but she's married to a white man and her white name is Missus Catherine Sutton. She's a fine-looking lady.

Imagine. Going all the way to England, which I hear tell is all the way on the other side of the world, and talking to the Queen!

Tuesday, August 11*th*, 1863

Strangest thing. Noah came round today and he was acting peculiar. I couldn't figure out what was wrong with him, but he wouldn't hardly talk to me at all. It wasn't until I got out my workbooks and asked him if he wanted to read with me that I found out what was going on.

"You sure you wouldn't rather be visiting with your white friend?" he asked, in an uppity tone of voice.

I do believe he's jealous!

His folks have got a piece of land to farm, but they're not going to move onto it until next spring. They've built a little shanty there and they're going to clear the land this fall, but they'll spend the winter here in town, then build a proper cabin after the snow goes. People tell us there's a powerful lot of snow here in the winter.

Mister Long and Noah's brothers think they'll be able to get jobs in a lumber camp for the winter. Noah and I'll be going to school together soon. Maybe that will make him feel better. In the meantime, I promised to go out to the land with him and help him pick stones. There are an awful lot to clean away, and bush to clear, before they can plant anything next spring.

Thursday, August 13th, 1863

I saw the most amazing thing today. Amelia came over real early and called me out. "A circus is coming to town," she shouted. "There's a parade! Come and see it!"

I ran out and of course Joseph ran out with me. I told Boze to stay home, but for once he didn't mind me. We ran down to Poulett Street. There was already a big crowd gathered there.

At first there was nothing to see, but then we heard music and down the street it came. First off there was a whole orchestra standing in a really strange kind of wagon — a chariot, someone said they called it — pulled by a team of the most beautiful horses I ever saw. They were a lovely honey colour, with pale yellow manes and tails. They pranced along as if they knew how beautiful they were. The chariot was painted golden and shone in the sun so bright it almost hurt my eyes, and the music the men were playing just set my feet to tapping. Before I knew it, Joseph had run out onto the street and was dancing along beside it. Then a whole bunch more horses and ponies in all different colours came trotting along. There were ladies in sparkly dresses riding on some of them, and some of the ladies were actually standing on the horses as they trotted by, waving their arms in the air. Don't know how they didn't fall off.

Then a big horse came along all by itself and a boy was jumping up and down off of it as it pranced along. A minute later another boy behind him was doing back flips on his horse! I've never seen the like of it.

Just as they were going by, wouldn't you know it, Boze ran out, barking. I tried to call him back, but two more dogs ran out to join him. I called to Joseph to catch Boze, but he didn't want to hear me. He only wanted to see those horses close up. A lot of other boys were running alongside the performers, too, and all in all, with the music blaring away, and folks cheering and applauding, it made quite a ruckus. The performers didn't seem to mind, though, or the horses. Guess they're used to it.

Then there were a whole lot of baggage vans — I guess they put the horses and ponies in them when they're moving from place to place. They were all painted and decorated up. At the very end some horses were doing a kind of skittering dance, and doing little jumps as they went along.

Then a man came along leading a mule. The mule had a sign on it saying it was the COMIC MULE SAM PATCH. When they got in front of us, the man suddenly stopped and the mule kept right on going. Ran into the back of him and knocked him down. Then he got up and I thought he was yelling mad at the mule, but turned out it was all part of the show and everybody watching was laughing at them. The man looked to be going to beat the mule with a stick, but the mule just grabbed the stick in his mouth, pulled it right out of the man's hand, and started in to waving it at him instead. Then they both ran off to catch up to the parade.

Amelia says her mother is going to take her and her

sisters to the show tonight. I would love to go too, but we can't afford it and I know my mama wouldn't let them pay for me. They didn't actually offer, anyway.

At least I saw the parade.

Friday, August 14th, 1863

Picking stones is hard work! But I said I'd help, so I will. Mister Long drove us out in the wagon to their piece of land early this morning and we worked all day. It's just to the north of Owen Sound, not too far away. It's up on a hill and there's a pretty view of Georgian Bay. Missus Long fixed a good lunch for us to take with us, and I was glad to stop and eat it. Luckily, there's a good stream on the property so we had lots of water to drink. It was blazing hot, though, and I've got blisters on my hands. Had to hide them so Noah wouldn't see. He'd have felt bad. His hands are tougher than mine and he doesn't get blisters.

Going back tomorrow.

Saturday, August 15th, 1863

I never want to see another stone in my life. Mister Long and Noah's brothers have cleared a big enough patch so that they can put up their tent, and they're going to set it up next week and stay up there. I feel bad that I won't be able to help anymore, but kind of relieved, too. A few more days like these past two and I don't think I'd have any skin left on my hands at all.

Noah and Missus Long are going to come back to their cabin here at Mister Frost's when school starts next week. His papa and brothers will stay on the farm and work at clearing it until the snow comes, then they're going to get jobs in a lumber camp.

Mama made me a new dress out of cloth that Missus Frost gave her in exchange for her ironing work. I am going to look mighty fine on my first day of school.

Monday, August 17th, 1863

Where to start? I love school. Amelia is in my class, and so is Noah. He and his mama are back here now. My teacher's name is Miss Wilson. Even though there's lots of coloured folk in Owen Sound, there's not so many coloured children here as there were in the school in Toronto. In fact, Noah and I are the only ones in our class. Miss Wilson is nice, though. She was impressed with how well I could read. I'm going to work as hard as I can.

Monday, August 24th, 1863

Amelia and I have been climbing on the rocks whenever we can, except for one day when it rained. That day we stayed in at her house and her mother gave us milk and cookies. I am developing a fondness for those molasses cookies.

Climbing on the rocks is exciting. I like it best when we get right up to the top and can look down over the city and the river, and right out to the harbour. Today we saw Amelia's daddy's steamer come in. Must be mighty fine to have a daddy who's a ship's captain. Not that my papa isn't just as fine a man. He's already got a reputation at the stables where he works. I heard a man talking about him the other day. "You got a problem with your horse," he was saying, "you just talk to Moses Jackson over at Cooper's stables. Isn't anything that man doesn't know about horses."

Guess that's where Joseph gets it from.

Friday, September 4th, 1863

I had a nice day today. Amelia and I went into town after school and we went to Granny Taylor's store. Granny Taylor sells apples and oranges and candies in a little store near the 8th Street bridge on the Sydenham River, close to the Market Square. Granny Taylor is a real cheery person. She gave us each an apple and a sweet. She threw a scrap to Boze, too. Her store is like a little bit of Paradise. She's got pies and fruit and cakes and cookies — the whole place smells so good it just got my mouth to watering and my stomach to growling. I've seen her at our church. Everybody there knows her. And likes her, too, by the looks of it.

When we left her store, I heard a great bell ringing. At first I didn't know what was going on, but Amelia grabbed me by the hand and pulled me down the street.

"It's Daddy Hall," she said. "He's our Town Crier. Come on, let's hear what news he's got today."

Along came a coloured man, swinging a hand bell and calling out announcements. He was telling about sales of sheep and lambs and I don't know what all. I didn't understand all of what he was saying, but he had such a strong fine voice it was pure pleasure to hear him. We followed him all the way along the street back to the Market Square. He ended his announcements there and called out "God Save the Queen!" real loud. Then he turned to us and called us over. I was so mortified I could hardly bring myself to go, but Amelia just dragged me over.

"Well now, Amelia," he said to her, and stooped down to scratch Boze behind the ears. "I see you've been following me around as usual. How are you today and who's your new friend?"

"Her name's Julia May," Amelia answered, not shy at all. "Her family just got here a while back. Escaped all the way from Virginia, they did."

"Well now," Daddy Hall said again. "That's just fine. Welcome, Julia May. I hope you're going to like Owen Sound."

I couldn't find my voice but I finally managed to squeak out a "thank you" to him.

"You all going to school?" he asked then.

Amelia told him we were before I could get another word out. "We're going together. We're in the same class."

He nodded. "Good for you," he said. "Education's a mighty fine thing. Make sure you learn to read, now."

"I already can," I blurted out, then bit my lip.

"Then you're well on your way," he said. He gave me a pat on the shoulder and looked over to where a young girl was standing. He said it was his daughter, Elizabeth, come to fetch him home for supper. We waved to her and she waved back, then they both went off up the hill.

Amelia told me he lives on the Pleasure Grounds. He was a slave, too, and escaped up here and has been the Town Crier for as long as she can remember.

When I came back to our cabin for my supper, Mama had fixed fried chicken. My very favourite. After supper we sat outside until it got dark. The fireflies were out and making sparks all over the garden. It was so peaceful, I felt something inside me go all soft.

Yes, Daddy Hall, I am going to like Owen Sound. I am going to like it just fine.

Friday, September 11*th*, 1863

So much going on! Sometimes it's hard to find time to write in this journal. When I get home from school I like to go over the work I did during the day. Amelia laughs at me and says I'm taking things too seriously, but I want to learn as much as I can. Miss Wilson says I'm like a sponge, just soaking everything up. Noah understands. He comes over and studies with me. I'd better be careful — he bested me at the spelling bee today! We two are the best spellers in the class.

Monday, September 14th, 1863

Amelia and I went back to the rocks after school today. The weather's been too drizzly lately, but today was sunny and dry. I wanted to ask Noah to come with us, but he was sort of quiet and said he couldn't. Something's bothering him, I think.

Boze came with us, though. He always does. He just sits and waits at the bottom of the cliff. That is one devoted dog. He's so funny. At first he was determined to go to school with me, but Miss Wilson didn't take to a dog sitting outside the door all day. I had to make him stay back, but Mama says somehow he knows when it's time for me to come home from school. He'll be sleeping away, then suddenly his ears will prick up and he'll jump up and trot off down the street. When I turn the corner he's always sitting there in the middle of the road, waiting. Wagons and carriages have to go around him. He won't move for anything.

Tuesday, September 15th, 1863

A terrible thing happened today. Noah got in a fight with a white boy from our class. He wouldn't tell me what it was about. He just got angry — I've never seen him like that before. The other boy told Miss Wilson that Noah started it, and when she asked him if that was true he wouldn't answer her, so he got the strap. Miss Wilson looked to be as angry as he was.

Monday, September 21st, 1863

I don't know what is going on with Noah, I truly don't. He got in a fight again today with another white boy. He still wouldn't say a word, and he got the strap again. Miss Wilson says if he gets into one more fight she's not going to let him come back to school.

I am trying to talk to him about it, but he just snaps at me to hush up and leave him alone.

There's no call for him to treat me like that.

Wednesday, September 23rd, 1863

Well, Noah did get into another fight. This time with two boys at once, and he certainly didn't get the better of it. His face is all beat up and one eye is swollen shut. You'd think Miss Wilson would feel a little sorry for him, but she doesn't seem to. Just told him if he couldn't behave better than that, to get out and not come back, so he stomped off home. It doesn't seem to occur to her that the other boys were fighting, too, but I guess they just say Noah started it, and he won't talk, so she believes them. That's the easiest thing for her to do, I reckon.

I don't think I like her as much as I did.

I ran over to his cabin as soon as school let out, but he wasn't there. Missus Long looked to have been crying and she told me Noah had gone to the farm. Said he told her he was finished with school and he was going to go and stay with his papa and his brothers.

"Oh, Julia May," she said, "he's talking about going to the lumber camp with them this winter, too. He's too young for that! I did so much want him to get schooling while he had the chance."

I comforted her best as I could, but in my heart I'm so angry with him. Why did he have to get himself into such trouble? Whatever possessed him?

Thursday, September 24th, 1863

Well, I know now what possessed him and I'm feeling about as terrible as I could. What kind of a friend am I, anyway, not to know that Noah wouldn't fight without a reason? I'm just as bad as Miss Wilson.

When I got to school today those boys who fought with Noah were all standing together in a bunch and laughing to beat the band. "Guess we settled that boy's hash," they said, only the word they used wasn't "boy." It was a word I haven't heard since we left Virginia and I'm not going to repeat it here.

"Guess we got rid of him good and truly," they said.

At that, I couldn't hold my tongue one minute longer. I just lit into them. Didn't use any cuss words, but I gave them a tongue-lashing that would have done Mama proud. They were so surprised that they didn't say a thing at first, then one of them picked up a stone. I decided I'd better get out of there, so I did.

I thought about telling Miss Wilson, but I decided not to. I don't think Noah would have wanted me to. It's too shameful. That's likely the reason why he wouldn't say anything in the first place. I miss him, though, and I am vicious angry that he can't go to school. He's smarter than half the boys in that class. Guess they know it, too. Probably another reason why they hate him. They can't bear to be shown up by a coloured boy.

But I hope he'll come back. I want him to come back.

Friday, September 25th, 1863

That fool dog can climb trees! I'm fond of climbing myself, but never thought he'd do what he did today. There's a lovely big tree down by the river that has a bend in it just within reaching distance of the ground. I like to sit there and watch the water. Usually Boze just sits on the ground below me, but he whines a bit and doesn't like it. Today didn't he give a mighty leap and land up there beside me! I had to grab hold of him to keep him from going right over and falling off the other side. I was going to shunt him back down again, but he looked so happy sitting there with me, tail wagging hard, that I just let him be. Now I suppose he'll want up every time I sit there.

Saturday, September 26th, 1863

Amelia's daddy showed me all around his steamer today. It's an elegant boat. Got a dining room and a place he calls a salon with big chairs covered in red velvet, and fancy tables and wood panelling on the walls. Even got rooms with bunks for passengers to sleep in. Amelia was pointing things out as much as he was. Acted like she owned the whole boat.

Sometimes she is a bit too prideful.

Monday, September 28ᵗʰ, 1863

Guess Boze isn't so much of a fool dog after all. In fact, he's a hero. Today was a really nice day. Sunny and bright, but the air had a kind of crispness in it that I never felt in the air down home. People keep telling me I'm going to hate the winter here, it's going to be so cold, but I like it so far. The leaves on the trees are turning all kinds of bright red and yellow colours. Looks like somebody painted them with all the brightest colours in their paintbox.

Anyway, it was just the right kind of day to go down to the river and sit on my tree and look at the water after school let out. I set off with Boze, but didn't realize Joseph was following me. I thought he was back with Mama, but she had shooed him out of the cabin and instead of finding a friend to play with, he decided to go with me. I didn't know anything about it until I heard a kind of cry from upriver a bit. There's a log there for people to go across on, and don't you know Joseph had to try to cross over on it, and fell in. When I saw him he was being swept down toward me. He can't swim, of course, and was just flailing around.

I panicked. I can't swim either, but I was just about

to jump down off my tree into the water anyway, to try and catch him as he went past, when Boze took off in a giant leap and landed square beside Joseph with an enormous splash. For a moment all I could see was water spraying everywhere and Joseph thrashing around and Boze thrashing around, and then Joseph grabbed onto the dog and thank the Lord had the sense to stop struggling. Boze is a pretty big dog and he just turned toward the shore and swam back, towing Joseph along with him.

I waded out and grabbed Joseph and hauled him in. By this time he was crying fit to beat the band. You'd think he was wailing about being near drowned, but it wasn't about that at all.

"Don't tell Mama!" he kept crying. "Don't tell her! She'll paddle me for sure!"

So I didn't. We stayed away until his clothes dried out a bit, then went back and I didn't say a thing. Mama's used to him coming home wet and dirty, so she didn't notice anything wrong. I gave that boy a talking to, but don't know if it did a mite of good. Probably not.

I'd love to tell Mama what a hero Boze was, but I can't. I'll tell Amelia at school tomorrow.

Dogs seem to have more common sense than folks.

How come they can just naturally know how to swim and people don't?

Tuesday, September 29th, 1863

Amelia was impressed when I told her what Boze did. She thinks he should get a medal. So do I, but we can't tell, so he won't. Mind you, if Joseph gets to riling me too much, I can threaten him with it. Maybe that might make him mind a bit more.

Wednesday, September 30th, 1863

Something happened at school today. I've been worrying it over in my mind and getting angrier and angrier. Miss Wilson was complimenting me on my spelling. Since Noah's gone, there's nobody who can come near me in spelling now. I was feeling pretty happy over it. "Maybe someday I'll be a teacher like you," I said.

Then she got this funny look on her face. "Oh, Julia May," she said back, "you couldn't possibly . . ."

Then she shut her mouth tight and got all red in the face. She was so embarrassed, I got embarrassed, too, so I didn't say anything more, but I've been thinking and thinking on it. What did she mean? Why couldn't I possibly? Because I'm coloured, is that why? Don't they let coloured girls be teachers? Don't they let girls who've been slaves be teachers? Would the white people not want a coloured girl teaching their children?

Come to think of it, I never did see a coloured teacher, not even in Toronto. They were all white.

I'm mad as a hornet, but got nowhere to let it out. Not about to tell Mama. She'd like to go and give that teacher a piece of her mind, she would.

Mama's been acting strange lately, anyway. All happy one moment, then tired and fussed the next. I'm not going to give her anything more to trouble herself about.

Friday, October 2nd, 1863

I told Amelia what Miss Wilson said. I thought she'd be as mad about it as I am. Instead she just said, "Why would you want to be a teacher, anyway?" We were eating her mother's good molasses cookies, and her mother was standing right there. Missus Pearce didn't say a word, but her face did. Seemed plain to me that she agreed with Miss Wilson. I choked on a cookie and had to get right out of there.

Well, today something nice happened at church. We just finished singing the first hymn when Father Miller held up his hand and announced he had something to say. Then he told everybody that there was a girl with a fine voice in the congregation and he wanted everyone to hear it.

He meant me! I near died when he beckoned me to come up beside him. "Sing the next hymn all by yourself, girl," he said.

I looked out at all those people and just prayed the floor would open and swallow me up. "I can't!" I said, but it came out no more than a squeak.

"You most certainly can," he said. "Come along now, I'll start you off."

Missus Leland started playing away on "There Is a Balm in Gilead," Father Miller boomed out the first words, and I couldn't do anything but join in.

The Lord must have been listening and took pity on me, because after the first couple of lines I just forgot all about everybody else and sang for the pure joy of it. Wasn't until I finished that I realized I was singing all by myself. Like to died, then, but the whole congregation started in to clapping and I could see Mama and Papa just beaming with pride. Even little Joseph looked impressed.

I'm feeling a lot better today.

Monday, October 5th, 1863

I found out what's the matter with Mama. She's going to have a baby! I'm going to have another sister or brother. And this one won't be born a slave! My new baby sister or brother will be born FREE. Nobody will ever be able to sell this child away from my Mama. This baby's going to be the first free person in our family! Except for our ancestors in Africa, I guess.

Miss Wilson was talking about ancestors. Everybody in the class has ancestors that come from countries like Ireland or England or Scotland. I told them my ancestors came from Africa and they weren't slaves. Not sure anyone believed me, though. Miss Wilson looked like she didn't.

But my ancestors *did* come from Africa. And maybe one of them was even the daughter of an African chief, just like Old Man Henson's grandmother.

It could be.

But I didn't say it. They didn't want to hear it.

Saturday, October 10th, 1863

I saw Noah again today. It's market day and lots of people were in town to sell their vegetables and fruit. Mister Long didn't have anything to sell, but he had to pick up supplies. He and Noah turned up at Missus Long's cabin early this morning. While he went into town, I grabbed onto Noah and took him down to my tree by the river. I had so much to tell him.

First off, I apologized about being mad at him for leaving, but that didn't go so well. He seemed more shamed than anything else that I had found out what those boys were taunting him about, so I changed the subject right quick. Told him all about Boze rescuing Joseph and showed him where it happened. He was impressed with that. Gave Boze a good scratch behind the ears. Boze seemed to know he was being praised for doing something special and he got that silly doggy grin on his face and just about wagged himself inside out.

I wasn't going to tell him what Miss Wilson said about me not being able to be a teacher, but somehow or other it just came out. I thought Noah wouldn't want to talk about that, either, but he surprised me.

"Know just how you feel, Julia May," he said. Then he got all flustered and started throwing stones into the water.

Made me feel good, though, to know somebody understands and cares about it.

Sunday, October 11th, 1863

Father Miller said we should have a special service today, seeing as how there were so many farmers in church, and the harvest had been so good this year. We all should give thanks, he said.

I certainly do give thanks that we are here.

And that Mama and Papa are happy and got work.

And that I got to see Noah again, but I wish he was going to stay. (Isn't *that* surprising?)

And that Amelia is my friend.

And that I'm good at school. (I had to put that in, no matter what Miss Wilson thinks.)

And that there's going to be a new baby. Can't hardly wait for that!

If only Thomas was here. And Sarah and Caleb and Daniel. I always think that, no matter how good things get, there's always that sorrow underneath it all.

Tuesday, October 13th, 1863

Mama just came back from visiting with Missus Long. She's feeling poorly, and sad about Noah and his papa going back to the farm. Sad that Noah's brothers didn't come in with them and she didn't get to see them at all. Mama says she's lonely, so she's going to keep her company as much as possible.

She told me Missus Long is going to have a baby, too, but she's keeping it a secret for now. Doesn't want Mister Long to worry about her.

There are lots of good people here who will help her out. One of the ladies says she's delivered a dozen babies and every one of them thrived. Missus Frost even came by with a big bowl of chicken stew for her. To keep her strength up, she said.

Friday, October 16th, 1863

Went for a long walk by myself in the woods down by the river today. It's starting to get cold, but not mean cold, just nice and brisk. The leaves on the trees are all set off by the bluest sky I ever did see, with soft, puffy white clouds scudding by. *Scudding* is my newest word. I'm glad I learned it already so I can use it to describe what those clouds were doing. It sounds exactly right

I can't believe it. Papa just brought home a *horse* for Joseph! Can't write more. Have to go out and see it and find out where it came from.

Joseph is running around like a wild boy.

Nothing new about that, though.

Monday, October 19th, 1863

The horse's name is Buck. He used to pull a wagon driven by a man named Sam Jones. Sam told Papa that the people he worked for said the horse was too old now, and he was afraid they were going to sell Buck to the knackers for horsemeat. Papa said Sam was just about crying when he told him that. Said he and that horse had been working together for twelve years. Papa said he couldn't stand seeing Sam so sad, so he just offered to buy the horse for whatever the knackers would have paid. It wasn't much, but I think Papa started worrying the moment he made the offer. Figured he couldn't go back on his word, though.

Mister Frost gave Papa permission to keep Buck in the field next to the cabins, and he can live in the stables in the winter, but Papa has to pay for his feed. I know Papa can't really afford that, but he got such a big smile on his face, watching Joseph hug that horse, that I know it was worth it to him. Mama thinks he's taken leave of his senses.

Boze has made friends with Buck already. Whenever he's not with me now, he's out in the field with that horse. Buck seems to like the company.

I don't need to describe how happy Joseph is.

And so is Sam. He comes around every now and then, just to lean on the fence and keep Buck company for a while.

Friday, October 23rd, 1863

Amelia and I went down to Granny Taylor's after school today. I didn't have money to buy any candy, but Granny Taylor gave us an apple each. Amelia wanted to buy sweets for me, but I wouldn't let her. She didn't understand that and got a little tetchy about it, even called *me* prideful, but I wouldn't give in.

Sometimes it's hard being her friend. She doesn't understand what it's like being a coloured girl, especially one who used to be a slave. She thinks because it doesn't matter to her, it shouldn't matter to me either. Fine for her, but she'll never have anybody tell *her* she can't be a teacher.

Daddy Hall came by just then, ringing his bell and calling out the news, and we tailed him to the Market Place, where he always ends up with his "God Save the Queen!" I thought I heard him say something about a battle in the war down in the United States, so I asked him about it. He told us it was a great victory for the North. That's really good news for the folks we left behind. I asked him did he know if any other coloured boys from here in Owen Sound were fighting down there, but he said he didn't think so. Some people called crimps came up a while back trying to recruit boys and promising to pay them to go fight, but far as he knew none went. I guess white people up here don't want to get mixed up in that war, and slaves who made it this far north sure don't aim to let their boys go back.

Wish Thomas hadn't gone. I wonder if he was in that battle. I said a little prayer right then and there for his safety.

Saturday, October 24th, 1863

Amelia and I spent the afternoon climbing on the rocks. It was the most glorious day! I never in my life thought leaves could turn the colours that the leaves on these trees hereabouts do. The maple trees are all scarlet (new word, but it just means really really red) and orange, and the birches are so brilliantly yellow that it looks like they're making their own sunshine. *(Brilliantly* is an adjective — a word that tells you what something's like. Most kids in my class aren't too interested in grammar, but I love it. Love to know how things work, including words.)

Miss Wilson likes it that I'm so good at school, I can tell, but she doesn't say too much about it. Doesn't want me to get my hopes up, I guess. She talked about everyone knowing their place in God's creation the other day, and she looked straight at me. What I want to know is who told her where my place in God's creation is. She got a direct connection to Heaven?

Tuesday, October 27th, 1863

I guess it had to happen. Joseph decided he wanted to ride Buck. Buck is not a riding horse, he's a wagon-pulling horse. Never had anybody try to get up on him before. I saw Joseph leading him over to where there was a big stone in the corner of the field, but I didn't know what Joseph was intending to do until it was too late. He lined Buck up beside the stone, then climbed up on it and jumped over onto Buck's back. Must have startled the poor horse no end. Anyway, Buck lived up to his name. Who would have ever thought an old horse like that could kick up the way he did? Of course, Joseph flew off and hit the ground with a thud.

Boze ran over to him, but there wasn't anything the dog could do this time. I ran over, too, and picked him up. He wasn't crying, just seemed a little stunned. Buck looked at him out of the corner of his eye and I swear that horse was thinking, "You better not try that again!"

I got Joseph home, again promising not to tell Mama, and he doesn't seem any the worse for wear.

I sometimes wonder how that child is going to live to grow up.

Wednesday, October 28th, 1863

You never know what that little brother of mine is going to do next. Mister Frost lost a cow a few days ago. Someone left the fence to the field in back of his house open and his cow strayed. He's been looking for it ever since, even put a notice in the newspaper.

Well, when I came home from school today I saw Joseph walking out of the woods with a big red and white cow ambling along behind him. Mister Frost's cow! Joseph just herded the cow into the field, made sure the gate was shut, then went up to Sheldon Place to tell Mister Frost he'd brought the beast home. I asked him where in the world he had found her and he just said, "In the woods." Of course, he's not supposed to go in the woods alone, but somehow or other that got overlooked.

Mama was flabbergasted. She asked him how he had ever managed to get the cow to follow him home, but Joseph didn't seem too excited about that.

"I just patted her and asked her to follow me and she did," he said. "I think she was glad someone was there to show her how to get home." That boy certainly has a way with all animals, not just horses. Except, of course, when he's trying to ride a horse that doesn't want to be ridden. But I think he learned that lesson and respects Buck more now.

Mister Frost was mighty pleased. The cow is with calf and he was upset about losing her. He gave Joseph twenty-five cents for a reward! Mama gave him a few pennies to spend at Granny Taylor's, then put the rest away safe for him.

Thursday, October 29th, 1863

Amelia's daddy is in port this week. Her brother is all excited because Captain Pearce is going to let William sail with him when he goes out next week. When I was over at Amelia's today he couldn't talk about anything else. Amelia's mother was a bit fussed, though. I think she's worried about William going off on the boat. Amelia's two little sisters were bouncing around eating cookies and spreading crumbs all over the place, and begging to go, too, but of course that's just nonsense — Nell and Mary together are just about as much of a nuisance as Joseph is, but they don't get into so much trouble. They are pretty spoiled. My mama wouldn't let them get away with near as much as Missus Pearce does.

I think maybe I've been too quick to judge Amelia's mother, though. She's just done the nicest thing! I was over at their house after school today and I was teaching Amelia how to sing the words to some of the songs we sing in our church. Missus Pearce put her head in the door (Amelia has her own room!) and said she'd never heard a girl sing so nice. Then she invited me to come and sing this Sunday in their church. The white church! I was way too scared to do that, but Amelia persuaded me. She says she'll be right with me all the time.

Can't help feeling excited about it, but my stomach is already full of butterflies.

Sunday, November 1st, 1863

It was real hard to walk into that church with Amelia and her parents and her two little sisters and her big brother this morning, but the people were so nice! Mama had me dressed up fine and scrubbed so clean I squeaked, and the folks there made me welcome as could be. I sat beside Amelia and she held my hand all during the service. They do a powerful lot of kneeling and sitting and standing up, but Amelia told me what to do when. Their preacher is a nice man, but a little boring. I found myself drifting off and not listening to him too well sometimes. He went on for a long time, too. Talked a lot about Christian charity. For some reason, that made me squirm a bit. In spite of their kindness, I did feel out of place, being the only coloured girl there, but I loved the hymns. Didn't know them all, but I picked up the ones I hadn't heard before real quick.

When the preacher called me to come up front I

near to died, but Amelia gave my hand a squeeze and shooed me on my way and her mother nodded at me and smiled, so I just got up my nerve and went up. I looked out at all those white faces and my knees started to shake so bad I thought I was going to fall down, but once I started singing, the shaking stopped, the butterflies settled down, and I forgot to be scared. It's always like that. I sang "There Is a Balm in Gilead," and then they asked me to sing some more, so I sang "Swing Low, Sweet Chariot."

When I finished they didn't clap or anything — they don't clap in that church, Amelia said — but when the service was over and we went outside, all the folks came up to me and said how much they enjoyed my singing. They asked me were those slave songs and I said they were.

They want me to come back next Sunday! I'm going to ask Mama to come with me. She'll be so proud and I won't be near so scared with her there.

Wednesday, November 4th, 1863

Captain Pearce sailed this morning. William went with him. He'll be gone for about a month, this time, Missus Pearce says. She's none too happy, but she says she's resigned.

Thursday, November 5th, 1863

Weather's getting colder and nastier. We even had a bit of snow today, but Amelia says that's nothing. I can hardly believe there will be as much of it as she's telling me, though.

Missus Long says Mister Long and the boys have gone off to the lumber camp for the winter. Noah too. Guess she'll miss them something fierce. Her baby's due in April. It will be time for the spring planting, so they should be back by then. Mama says our baby's not due till May. Maybe if it's a girl we could call her Aleisha. I like that name.

I hope it's a girl. I could do with a sister. Not that she could ever replace Sarah, but it would be nice to have another girl in the family and I would love being a big sister to her. I would try to be just as good to her as Sarah was to me.

Saturday, November 7th, 1863

Going to Amelia's church again tomorrow. I'm glad Mama's going with me and I'm looking forward to it, but I'll be glad to get back to our own church next week. Feel more at home there.

Sunday, November 8th, 1863

I am so angry I can hardly write. So shamed I don't even want to write, but I have to do something and I don't know what else to do. I feel like there's a huge big fury building up inside me that is just going to *burst* out. One thing I do know. I am never, never, NEVER going back to Amelia's house. Never want to taste those molasses cookies Missus Pearce bakes again. I don't know if I can even bring myself to be friends with Amelia anymore. Know I don't want to see her right now.

Mama was so happy to be going to church with me this morning to hear me sing for the white folks. She dressed herself up more nicely than I ever did see.

I told Amelia I'd meet her at the church and she and her mother and sisters were there waiting for me. I felt right away something was wrong, but I couldn't figure out what. Missus Pearce wasn't nearly so nice as she usually is. I introduced Mama to her, but she didn't hardly say anything. I figured we must be late, although I didn't think we were, because she just hurried us in and didn't stop to talk to the other folks at all. Then she made us sit right at the back, not up at the front where we sat last week. Even Amelia was acting a little strange. I thought maybe they were just missing Captain Pearce and William.

The preacher called me up to sing at the end of the service and I went, but I only sang one song this time, "Follow the Drinking Gourd." No one asked me to sing another.

After church no one came round to say how much they liked it. Missus Pearce fairly yanked Amelia off without hardly even saying goodbye. I thought maybe they didn't like that song for some reason, but then I overheard Missus Pearce say something to one of the other ladies as she was going off. "Imagine. Bringing her mother here! Give them an inch and they'll take a mile," she said.

At first I didn't know what she meant. Then it sank in. Mama was standing right beside me and she heard it as plain as I did. Amelia turned round. I saw that she realized we had heard and her face got really red, but she turned back quick and went off with her mother without another look back. My face got so hot it felt like it was on fire. I didn't know what to do or where to look. Mama didn't say a word, just grabbed my arm and marched me off. She still won't talk to me, she's just cleaning up a storm in the cabin. Papa and Joseph don't know what's going on, but they're staying out of her way.

Monday, November 9th, 1863

Amelia tried to be nice to me at school today, tried to say she was sorry, but I just couldn't bring myself to let her. Couldn't even bring myself to look her in the face.

Friday, November 13th, 1863

Amelia keeps on trying to be nice. I almost feel sorry for her, but I just cannot be nice back.

Monday, November 16th, 1863

Snowing today. I think I see what everybody means! It started this morning. Sure was cold when I left for school. The snow was blowing and blowing in my face and I could hardly walk against the wind. I never knew snow could sting so hard. I had a scarf wrapped round my head, but any part of my face that it didn't cover was soon freezing. The schoolhouse was really cold, even though we kept a good fire going in the wood stove.

It just snowed and snowed. Finally Miss Wilson told us all to go home. I couldn't believe how deep it was when we went out. I had to slog through snow halfway up to my knees. Joseph, of course, just went crazy. He and his friends threw snowballs at each other all the way home, and pushed each other into the snowbanks. By the time we arrived at our cabin he was soaking wet and then he realized how cold he was and started crying. Mama had to fill up the washtub with hot water to thaw him out. Soon as he was warm and dry again, he was all for going out to see how Buck was. Mama wouldn't let him, of course, but when Papa came home he and Joseph went out to fetch the horse and they took him back to the stables. Then both Papa and Joseph were wet and freezing. Mama filled up the tub again and they took turns soaking in it.

I don't imagine there will be any school tomorrow either.

Looking out the window of our cabin, all I can see is swirling white snow. Now and then I can just catch a glimpse of the candle burning in Missus Long's cabin. Papa checked in on her and said she had a good fire going and was snug as a bug in a rug.

Saturday, November 21st, 1863

Snow's stopped and everything is glistening white out there. Joseph lit out of the cabin first thing this morning and he and his friends played out in the snow all day. The trees all have blobs of snow on them and the sky is as blue as can be. It's truly beautiful. And so quiet! Sounds like the whole world is muffled.

Amelia came round but I wouldn't talk to her. Mama said she looked worried and maybe I should see what was wrong, and that what happened wasn't her fault, but I wouldn't. Mama's more forgiving than I am.

Monday, November 23ʳᵈ, 1863

Back to school today but Amelia wasn't there. Found out why when I went home, and why she was worried yesterday. Captain Pearce's boat is missing! He was due into Collingwood when that storm blew up, but never made it.

Tuesday, November 24ᵗʰ, 1863

Missus Frost came round this afternoon after school, asking me if I had seen Amelia. Seems she's missing, too, and Missus Frost knows we're friends. Were friends, anyway. Now I feel guilty for being so mean to her. But I think I know where she might be. I'm going out to look for her.

I found her, but we both had a terrible time. I thought she might have gone up to the rocks to watch for her daddy's steamer. It's a dreadful time to be climbing there, with the snow and all, but I figured she might just be worried enough to try it. I didn't tell Mama what I was planning to do because it was already late and getting dark and I knew she probably wouldn't let me, but nobody else knows where we climb, so I had to go. I shut Boze in a shed out back. He got right indignant about that and started in to whining, but I didn't want him following me.

It was hard getting through the snow at the bottom of the rocks, and the rocks were so slippery and wet I was thinking twice about climbing them. Then I heard a voice calling out. It was Amelia. She sounded weak and sort of hopeless. I called back as loud as I could, then started up. It was harder climbing than I've ever done, but I finally got up to where she was, and I saw what the trouble was. She had fallen in a crack and her foot was all twisted and stuck in it. When I got up to her she was shivering and crying and in a terrible state.

"Oh, Julia May," she cried, "thank goodness you're here!"

I had to calm her down some before I could even start to help her get her foot out. She was hanging onto me and crying and crying.

"I just wanted to see if Daddy might be coming back into the harbour," she kept saying, over and over. "I just wanted to know he got through the storm safe."

Finally we got her loose, but then her foot hurt so much she couldn't put any weight on it. I had to half carry her back down. Didn't know if I could do it, but then I remembered Thomas carrying that old man so far and I figured if he could do it, I could, too. My heart was in my mouth the whole way, though, I was so scared of us both falling, but finally we managed to get to the bottom and wouldn't you know it, waiting down there was Boze. By that time it was pretty dark, but we know our way out of the bush. Besides, Boze knows the way even better. We just had to follow him.

Got back to her house and there was a pile of people there who had been out looking for her, too. Her mother was so glad to see her she just hugged and hugged her. Missus Pearce didn't hardly notice me at all. Everybody was so happy and excited, I just slipped away and came home without anybody noticing.

Mama sure noticed when I came back, though. Seems Boze barked and howled up a storm after I left, and when she let him out he just lit off. Then she realized I wasn't home. She and Papa asked around Missus Long's and all the other cabins, looking for me, and they were about to make up a search party of their own when I arrived. Mama was fit to switch me for going off without telling anybody, but when I told them what happened, Papa saved my hide.

"She's back safe and sound," he said. "And she found that little girl. Let her be."

Later

We just heard that Captain Pearce's boat made it into Collingwood safely. Seems he chose to ride the storm out on Nottawasaga Bay, which was the best thing to do.

Wednesday, November 25th, 1863

Amelia wasn't at school today. Miss Wilson said she caught a chill yesterday.

Thursday, November 26th, 1863

Amelia is still not back at school.

Friday, November 27th, 1863

Amelia came back to school today. I was glad she wasn't taken real sick. After school we went to sit down by the river on my tree, even though it was pretty cold. We had to talk.

First off, Amelia started crying and apologizing for what her mother said, then she got into thanking me for finding her and getting her home. It all got complicated. Finally I said, "Let's forget it. Let's just be friends again."

She seemed happy about that. Asked me to go home with her for milk and cookies, but I could not do that. "We'll be friends," I said, "but I can't go back to your house."

"Can't you forget what my mother said?" she asked me, but I said I couldn't.

Then she said that a good Christian can forgive sins people do against them, and I said they could only forgive if the person who hurt them was sorry and apologized, and I didn't see her mother doing that. In fact, she hadn't even thanked me for bringing Amelia home. Then Amelia said I was being hard and cruel, and I said she didn't understand anything, and she jumped down from the tree and ran home, and I ploughed through the snow back here, and we're not speaking again.

Monday, November 30th, 1863

Mama saw an advertisement in the newspaper today for a sewing machine. She has always been handy with a needle and she thinks if she had a machine like that she could take in sewing instead of laundry. It would be a lot easier work and earn her more money, too. She cut out the advertisement and showed it to me, but it costs twelve dollars. She knows we can't possibly afford it, but she says she's going to try and start saving up for it. It hurts me to see how badly she wants that machine.

Tuesday, December 1st, 1863

A terrible thing! Noah was brought home from the lumber camp to Missus Long's cabin — the one here in Owen Sound, not the one out at their farm. He's been hurt bad. Cut his leg with an axe. Papa told me tonight. I'm going to go over to see him first thing after school tomorrow.

Wednesday, December 2ⁿᵈ, 1863

I couldn't sleep for worrying about Noah last night. I've heard so many stories about men getting hurt bad in the lumber camps and even dying. I couldn't wait to go see him after school, so I went over early this morning. He was lying on a straw pallet beside the hearth. One leg was all bandaged up, and even from the doorway I could see blood all dried up on the dressing. Noah was lying with his eyes closed when I got there, but he wasn't sleeping. Missus Long told me in a whisper that he couldn't sleep a wink, the pain was so bad. She went over and gave his shoulder a little squeeze, to tell him I was there. He opened his eyes then and looked at me and I've never seen anybody look so awful. His face was tight with pain. He tried to give me a smile, but it just came out a contortion. It was all I could do not to bust out crying.

It got worse.

Missus Long told me that the doctor at the camp had bandaged up his leg, but the men who carried him here told her the doctor said she had to change the dressing when Noah got here. She asked me to help.

I held Noah's hand while Missus Long unwrapped the bandages. She was as careful as could be, but even so Noah just screamed out. When I saw the wound, I near fainted. The doctor had said it wasn't too bad and would heal, but it looked dreadful. It was red and puffy, and stitched together with what looked like thread. Right in the middle of his leg, just above the knee.

Missus Long gave Noah a piece of leather and told him to bite down on it hard. I soon saw why. The doctor had sent her a bottle of carbolic acid and told her to wash the wound with it before she put a new dressing on. When she poured it over the wound Noah made the most horrible sound, even though his teeth were tightly closed around the leather strip. Tears just poured down his cheeks. He held my hand so hard it's all bruised.

When she had finished and bound the wound up again, Missus Long sat back and I saw she was shaking all over. "Thank the Lord we don't have to do that again for five days," she said. She gave Noah a hug and went to see to the fire.

I just sat there with Noah. After a while he seemed to sleep, so I got up, careful not to wake him, and went off to school.

Went back after school. Noah is still sleeping. I'll go back again tomorrow.

But I can't help thinking, what if Thomas is wounded bad like Noah and lying in some tent somewhere with no family to see to him?

Oh, how I wish this war would end and he would come home!

Thursday, December 3rd, 1863

Noah was sitting up and looked a bit better today. I sat with him until suppertime.

Saturday, December 5th, 1863

Noah is a bit better.

Sunday, December 6th, 1863

I said a little prayer for Noah at church today.

Monday, December 7th, 1863

I helped Missus Long change the dressing again today. Thank the good Lord the wound is healing well, although it still pained Noah something terrible while we were doing it.

Tuesday, December 8th, 1863

I took my reader over to Noah today. Thought it would do him good to get back to work. He was grateful, but he says he won't go back to school. He won't be going back to the lumber camp either, thank goodness, but he's going to go out to the farm when his father and brothers come back in the spring.

I can't blame him. I know they'll need him to work the land and do the planting, but it is a waste. He won't be up and walking for a time, though, so I'll make sure he doesn't forget his letters. I know Missus Long is happy to have him back here with her for the winter. She told him about the new baby coming in the spring and he was glad about that. He'll be a help to her this winter once he's up and about.

Wednesday, December 16th, 1863

It's my birthday today! When I came into the kitchen for breakfast, there was a wrapped parcel sitting on the table at my place. It was new boots! I admit I needed them, as my feet get powerful cold with the snow here. I gave Mama and Papa a big hug to thank them. I don't know how they could afford them, but somehow they did. I thought of Mama wanting that sewing machine so much, and I'm very afraid she used the money she was saving up for it on those boots. When I started to ask, though, she just gave me another extra-special-hard hug.

"Don't you worry your mind about that," she said. "You need boots, you're going to have them."

Then Mama made us a stew with a rabbit that Papa trapped. It was so good! Mama told me to take some over to Missus Long and Noah, so I did after supper. Wearing my new boots.

I do feel truly loved.

Can't help remembering one thing, though. On my birthdays when I was little, before she got sold off, Sarah used to scoop me up into her lap, wrap her arms around me, and sing a special birthday song just for me.

There. Now I've made myself cry. I'll stop this minute. It's been a lovely day and I won't spoil it.

Going to say a special prayer for Sarah instead.

Sunday, December 20ᵗʰ, 1863

The most amazing thing. Amelia turned up at our church this morning. I couldn't believe it when I saw her standing there at the back. She looked real shy, so I went and sat beside her. When I asked her whatever possessed her to do such a thing, she just said that she was sorry for what she said and she wanted to be friends again. She said I was never to home when she came over, and I wouldn't talk to her at school, so she decided to come to our church. She just snuck over before their own church service.

I guessed Missus Pearce would have a fit if she knew that Amelia had come to the coloured church and I asked her what she would do if her mother found out. She just raised her eyebrows like her mother does and said, "I'll cross that bridge when I come to it," and we both burst out laughing. That's one of Missus Pearce's favourite sayings and Amelia sounded just like her.

Father Miller looked hard at us and we managed to stop laughing, but we both had little smiles on our faces for the rest of the service. I wanted her to stay and meet Father Miller, but she didn't dare. She just slipped out fast when the service ended.

Who would have ever thought she would do such a thing? That was real brave on her part. The white folks would definitely not approve. I guess Amelia really is a good friend. I'm glad she is, and I don't want to fight with her ever again, no matter what her mother says or does.

Monday, December 21ˢᵗ, 1863

School's over until the new year and we're getting ready for Christmas. Our first Christmas in Canada. Our first Christmas as free folk, not slaves!

Tuesday, December 22ⁿᵈ, 1863

Us children from the cabins helped Mister and Missus Frost with decorating their house. We cut pine branches and brought them back, and Missus Frost has them over the fireplace and all around the stairs. It looks real pretty. Then they brought in a huge pine tree. In Virginia, our Master and Missus Jackson used to decorate up the Big House at Christmas and have great parties, and they sent round leftover food from the Big House after Christmas Day, but there was never very much of it. Mister and Missus Frost are different. They invited all of us who are living in their cabins to come by on Christmas Eve after church. It will be really special.

Wednesday, December 23ʳᵈ, 1863

It's snowing again. More than before. I haven't dared set toe outside the cabin, even with my new boots. The wind is howling and the snow is swirling around so bad I can't see our outhouse. Guess we'll use the buckets until this is over. I know I'm not going out in it.

Thursday, December 24th, 1863

Christmas Eve! The snow has stopped and the sun came out. The sky was so blue this morning I couldn't believe it, and the snow was pure white and sparkling so much I couldn't even look at it without squinting. Joseph, of course, was going crazy, wanting to get out and play in it, and some of the other children were hooting and hollering out there, throwing snow around at each other, so I bundled him up as best as I could and put just about all the clothes I own on me, and out we went. Mama has relented and let Boze sleep in the house because it's so cold, so he came out, too. He tore around in a frenzy, biting snow and rolling and burying his whole face in it, then coming up snorting. I threw snowballs for him and he caught them in his teeth, then shook his head in surprise when the snow sprayed all over him. Then the children threw snow at me, and I threw snow back at them. I forgot my dignity completely and just played. It was fun.

I left Joseph with his friends and made my way over to the Longs'. Noah was sitting by the window, just staring out.

"Did you ever see the like of this?" I asked, but he just grinned at me.

"Snows like this in Ohio every winter," he said. "You're just a soft little Southern gal."

I was about to get riled, then I saw he was only teasing me and I laughed, too. It was good to see him feeling so fine.

We're going to church tonight, then over to Mister and Missus Frost at Sheldon Place. I'm excited, but mixed in with that is a lot of sadness. I wonder where Thomas is. Not much celebrating on Christmas Eve when you're fighting a war, I expect.

Saturday, December 26th, 1863

Well, we had a fine Christmas, in spite of our sadness. We went to church on Christmas Eve. There wasn't a moon, and even though the stars were shining more bright than I've ever seen them, it was deep dark, and we had to carry a lantern with us. The snow crunched under our feet as we walked, and it was so cold it was fierce, but our little church was good and warm inside. Father Miller had the wood stove going and the church was packed with people. Christmas is such a family time, though, I couldn't stop thinking about Thomas, and wondering where Sarah, Daniel and Caleb were. I prayed so hard that they might be having as good and safe a Christmas as we were, but I couldn't make myself believe they were. Mama and Papa were so quiet, and their faces were so still, I knew they were thinking the same thing.

After the service we walked through the snow up to Sheldon Place. The house was all lit up with candles in every window. Missus Frost invited us all right inside and gave us a cup of hot cider. There were white people and coloured folk all there together, everyone wishing everyone else a Happy Christmas. Gave me a warm glow inside. They had that big tree decorated up with every manner of trinket and decoration. Had candles burning on every branch. I held tight to Joseph so he couldn't get near it, though. I could just see him knocking one of those candles off and setting the whole place on fire.

Mama brought some of her fine cornbread as a present, and Missus Frost was pleased. She said she liked nothing better than cornbread and she was looking forward to enjoying it. Mama was happy about that. Before we left, a group of carollers came to the door. They sang so beautifully, I got tears in my eyes.

Missus Frost sent home a chicken with every one of us families from their cabins. Mama boiled it up for our dinner tonight with dumplings. Just before it was ready, there was a knock at the door. It was Missus Long and Noah. Mama had invited them, but Missus Long wasn't sure whether Noah would be able to make it or not. If he hadn't, I would have taken some chicken and dumplings over to them, but there they were. Missus Long said the smell of our chicken cooking was so good that nothing could have kept Noah away. She brought a pudding like they used to make in Ohio. All full of plums and raisins. It was delicious. We had a feast!

This has been the best Christmas I have ever had, but, oh, Thomas, I wonder where you are.

1864

Friday, January 1ˢᵗ, 1864

A new year! I wonder what it will bring us. A new baby, I know that. Mama is busy sewing blankets and clothes for it and I'm helping, but I'm not very good at sewing. Things I make turn out lumpy.

I wonder if it's too much to hope for that the war in the United States ends and Thomas comes home safe. It probably is. I'm going to pray for it anyway. Daddy Hall says the news is not very good for the South. That gives me a little more hope about our Thomas.

Monday, January 4th, 1864

What a day! Amelia came over and invited me to go skating on the Mill Pond with her. At first I didn't see how I could do it, but she just insisted. She had an extra pair of skates and brought them over for me. I told her I couldn't skate, but she said that didn't matter a bit. She was going to teach me. I admit I was doubtful, but Mama shooed me out of the house and told me to go and enjoy myself. I was helping her sew things for the baby and she had to fix up so many of my tangles and knots I think she was anxious to get shut of me for a while, so between Amelia and Mama I didn't have much choice.

We went to the Mill Pond up behind the dam. It had frozen smooth and folks had shovelled all the snow off. We sat down and she showed me how to strap the skates onto my boots, then we stood up. I didn't stay standing for long, though. Those skates were the most awkward things I've ever had on my feet! Before I even got near the ice I fell down three times. Amelia helped me up, but she was laughing so hard she nearly fell down, too.

Getting onto the ice turned out to be the easy part. There was no way I could stand up on it. I just slipped, fell, crawled back up, then slipped, fell and crawled back up again. I would have given up ten times but Amelia just kept making me try again. Then some children from our class at school came over. They were white children — I'm the only coloured student in my class now that Noah is gone — but these ones were friendly and they decided to help. With Amelia hanging onto me on one side, and a girl named Kathleen hanging onto the other side, somehow or other I managed to stumble across the pond without falling. They weren't satisfied, though. Made me go back across again. And again. And again.

And do you know what? Suddenly I could do it all by myself! I couldn't slide along all smooth and fast like the others did, and I had to sort of take little bitty steps, but I did it. Didn't fall hardly at all after that.

We're going back tomorrow. Amelia says I'll be

skating good as her by the time winter's over.

Hard to believe, but I might!

Tuesday, January 5th, 1864

Went skating again today. I'm beginning to learn how to slide my feet.

Wednesday, January 6th, 1864

I can do it! I can skate! I'm sliding along good as Amelia, almost. Now I have to learn to go backwards. Haven't got that figured out yet.

Friday, January 8th, 1864

I can go backwards now, too. Amelia and I had a great time. We held hands and just swooped around that pond. I love it!

Boze isn't too happy about it, though. First day he tried to follow me out onto the ice, but he slipped all over and nearly got mixed up with a boy's skates. I was afraid he was going to get hurt, so I made him stay off the ice. Now he just sits at the edge and looks worried. When I come back to take my skates off, he near goes crazy with relief.

Saturday, January 9th, 1864

Just realized. It's nearly a year since we ran away. Seems like a whole lifetime. It was so brave of Mama and Papa and Thomas to run and especially to take us young ones with them. I know how much harder it made it for them to have Joseph and me holding them back. They could have left us with Auntie Sal and Bessie — running is so dangerous, some children's parents do leave the little ones with friends or relatives for safety's sake — but then they would be mourning us, and Joseph and I would still be slaves and we wouldn't ever know what had happened to them. Can't bear to think of that.

If only Thomas hadn't gone back.

Sunday, January 10th, 1864

We got some truly wonderful news!
MY SISTER SARAH IS FOUND!

I guess I better say she found us. I can't believe it, but she's in Toronto, staying with Missus Blunt. I'm so excited I can hardly

I had to sit back, take a deep breath, and begin at the beginning. Maybe even two deep breaths.

Good. Now I've collected myself.

Yesterday at church Father Miller came up to us, holding a letter. He said it was for us. We couldn't understand how someone could be writing to us, but he said it was from Reverend Brown in Toronto. Well, at first we were just plain terrified that it was bad news about Thomas. Mama took the letter from Father Miller and put it in her pocket.

"Thank you kindly," she said. "We'll read it when we get home after the service."

If you didn't know her, you would think she never gave that letter another thought all during the service, but I saw that her hand stayed in her pocket and her apron was shaking. Papa just got that grim look on his face and stared straight ahead the whole time. I don't think he heard a word of the service. I don't think any of us had any idea whatsoever what was going on in church this morning. Joseph, of course, never knows what's going on anyway, because he never pays attention. He didn't pay any mind to the letter and didn't realize it had to be important.

I usually like church, but this morning it was just plain torture trying to sit there, and the two hours before we got home were the longest two hours of my life. Finally we got in the cabin and Papa told us to sit down at the table. Then he told Mama to go ahead and open the letter. Mama didn't have time to learn to read too well in Toronto, so when she opened the letter she handed the pages to me. My hands were shaking so much I couldn't make the letters out at first.

The letter was from Reverend Brown. It started off with the words, *Dear Mister and Missus Jackson, I have wonderful news for you.*

When I read that, it was as if my whole body suddenly got light and my heart started beating again.

It went on to say that a young lady and her husband and baby had arrived in Toronto from Rochester, looking for us. Said her name was Sarah and she was my big sister. Reverend Brown told her he knew where we were. He settled her and her family in Missus Blunt's house and wrote to us right away. He didn't say any more about how they got there or how Sarah knew to follow us to Toronto, but I expect she'll tell us all that when she gets here.

WHEN SHE GETS HERE!

We sent a letter right back to Reverend Brown — I wrote it, but Mama and Papa told me what to say — telling Sarah that Papa would be there to fetch her as soon as possible. He's going to try to get the loan of a horse and sleigh. He has to go quick while the roads are frozen, so he can get back before the weather turns too mild. Once the roads thaw out in spring they'll be so muddy and bad he wouldn't be able to get there until they dry out in summer. We can't wait that long to bring Sarah and her family back up here to us and learn how she managed to find us.

And she has a baby! I'm an aunt!

Wonder what the baby's name is? Wonder if it's a girl or a boy? Wonder how old it is? Wonder what Sarah's husband is like and where she met him?

Wonder, wonder, WONDER!

Monday, January 11th, 1864

Back to school today. After school I went over to visit with Noah and tell him our good news. His Mama is sure glad to have him with her to help out. She's doing poorly. My Mama doesn't seem to have any problems at all carrying our new baby, but Missus Long seems to have one trouble after another. She was happy to hear about Sarah finding us, though. I took over some soup, but Missus Long was feeling too sickly to take more than a few sips of it.

Mama's worried about her. So is Noah. I sat with him for a while and tried to get him interested in reading some school books, but I could tell his mind wasn't on it, so I let him be.

Funny how I thought at first he was such a pesky boy.

Papa hasn't been able to get a horse and sleigh yet. Mama is near crazy with impatience, but he said he'd find someone who would lend him one for the trip somewhere. Mister Cooper who owns the stables is helping him look, but he can't spare any of his horses or sleighs. They're all working up in the lumber camps.

Tuesday, January 12th, 1864

Sam came by today. Said he'd heard the news about Sarah. He said he could get us a sleigh, and he figured Buck was good for one more trip, so he and Papa are off to fetch Sarah tomorrow. Joseph is howling mad that they won't take him, but Papa says he will have enough to do to take care of Sarah and her family and they will have to travel fast. Joseph tried to say they couldn't take Buck, that Buck was his horse now, and he wouldn't give permission, but Papa put a stop to that talk real quick.

Wednesday, January 13th, 1864

Papa and Sam left today. Joseph is sulking. He was born after Sarah was sold off, so he doesn't know her and he doesn't realize what a wonderful thing it is that she's found. He'll see when she gets here, though.

Papa figured it would take about two weeks to get to Toronto, and another two weeks to get back here, travelling as fast as they could. Missus Long lent him their good tent and they'll stay in that on the way there if it's not too cold, but Papa's hopeful that they might find places that will take them in on the way back because of the baby. Fortunately, Papa has managed to save up enough money to pay for that — at least, he hopes so. Mama gave him the rest of the money she's been saving for the sewing machine, too. If they can't find a tavern or hotel that will let them in, though, or a coloured family like Mister and Missus Thornton, they'll just have to camp out and keep Sarah and the baby as warm as they can.

How am I going to wait a whole month to see them? I am more excited and happy than I have ever been in my whole life. Mama is going around singing!

I hope that old horse can make it.

Friday, January 15th, 1864

How can things be so happy one day, and so sad the next? I hadn't hardly finished writing that last entry when there was a knocking at the door. It was Noah! He had struggled through the snow to tell us his mama was having her baby! It's much too early. Mama went over to help her, and the doctor came, but Missus Long lost her baby.

I feel so bad for her. Noah was crying, though I pretended not to see.

Sunday, January 17th, 1864

We had a special service this morning for Missus Long and her baby. Mama's over with her now. I'm waiting for some stew to finish cooking, then I'm going to take it over.

Later

Folks have been so kind. There was so much food over at Missus Long's that she won't have to cook for a week. Just as well, because she's really looking poorly.

Monday, January 18th, 1864

I went over to Missus Long's after school today. Mama was with her most of the day, but she has a pile of washing and ironing to do so she had to go home.

I had to help her finish up and it took us until late tonight to do it. Too tired to write more now.

Tuesday, January 19th, 1864

Back to Missus Long's. She's a mite better, but still not doing too well. Noah is taking good care of her. I never knew that boy could be so gentle.

Wednesday, January 20th, 1864

Amelia came with me to Missus Long's. She never got to know Noah very well at school, and she was shy around him in his house, but he put her at her ease. She brought molasses cookies. I made like I didn't notice. Noah liked them, though. I guess I can't expect him to turn them down just because of my feelings. Besides, he doesn't know a thing about what happened at that church.

Amelia and Missus Long got on real well. Amelia has a good way about her with people who are feeling poorly. Quiet and kind. I never saw that side of her before.

Thursday, January 21st, 1864

Papa and Sam have been gone a week. Wonder how close they are to Toronto? Wonder how Sarah is doing?

More wondering! When will it stop? I am in a frenzy.

Monday, January 25th, 1864

Missus Long is finally getting her strength back, but now she is worried to death about Noah. That boy decided that since his mama is better, he had to be earning some money. I know they must need it, but his leg is hardly healed and he still limps something terrible. The whole bay has frozen over and he has gone and signed up to help cut ice out there. It's hard work, and it means handling a saw. Missus Long is fit to be tied.

Amelia and I went down after school today to watch. The men go away out on the ice and mark off where they're going to cut. Then they saw the ice into squares, haul it out with big ice tongs, and load the blocks onto sleds. There's a man there only has one arm because of an accident, but he can haul up ice blocks faster than anybody else. Those ice tongs they use are hinged, Noah says, so that you can do it with only one hand. It's a marvel to watch that man work.

They haul the loaded sleds back to a big ice house on the shore and pile it up there, with sawdust in between the blocks to keep them from sticking together or melting. Noah says the ice stays frozen in there until well into the summer. He's real proud to be working again. I have to say I'm proud of him, too.

Amelia and I went back to reassure Missus Long that he was taking care and he'd be all right.

I sure hope he will.

Wednesday, January 27th, 1864

Papa should be in Toronto by now.

Wednesday, February 3rd, 1864

I can't think of anything else but Sarah and her family. Are they on their way here yet? The weather has been good for travelling. No snowstorms, but cold enough so that the roads will be frozen and hard-packed. I wonder how Buck is holding up? Joseph is still mad as hops at not being allowed to go, and he's fretting about the horse. Makes me angry that he's not thinking about Sarah at all, but I guess that's only normal. He's so young, he's almost forgotten Thomas, although every once in a while he remembers and asks about him. Mama and Papa always reassure him and tell him Thomas is fine and will be home as soon as the war is over. Then he goes and starts playing war with his friends. That upsets me, but I tolerate it. Can't expect too much from him.

Friday, February 5th, 1864

Amelia and I went down to watch the ice cutting again today. That ice house is filling up fast. It's real cold in there. Noah says in summer it will be the coolest place in town.

Monday, February 8th, 1864

Now I'm worried about Mama. She just waves me off when I say anything, says she never had any problems carrying a baby before, but I can see that her back is hurting her and she sometimes has a hard time catching her breath. I'm coming straight home from school every day to help her with the washing. Joseph and I are toting the clean laundry back to her customers when it's done, same as we did in Toronto. That helps a bit.

If it gets to be too much of a trouble for her, I'll stay home from school and help out.

Wednesday, February 10th, 1864

I told Mama I was going to stay home from school today and she just about bit my head off. Said she was not going to let me miss my learning and she was just fine, thank you.

My Mama is a stubborn woman. Papa always says that, and he's right.

Almost a month since Papa left to fetch Sarah. It's fixing to storm tomorrow, they say.

Something else to worry about.

Friday, February 12th, 1864

Snowing hard. No sign of Papa and Sarah.

Monday, February 15th, 1864

Snow's cleared up and it's got a lot warmer. Now I am worried about the road breaking up.

Wednesday, February 17th, 1864

THEY'RE HERE! THEY'RE HERE!

Friday, February 19th, 1864

Oh, where do I begin? Sarah and her husband — that's Miles — and her baby — that's Liza — are here. I am in a daze of joy. And that's not all! I'm not going to get ahead of myself, though. I'm going to make myself tell everything just as it happened.

Snow started falling again on Wednesday, and Mama and I were worried. We neither one of us said anything, but we just kept looking out the window. I know we were both thinking the same thing. Where were Papa and Sarah, and how bad was the snow going to get? I flat out refused to go to school and stayed home to help with the washing. Mama did need the help but, truth to tell, I was too fussed to think about school. Then along about dinnertime, Boze started to bark. I flew to the door, and there was the sleigh pulling up in front of our cabin. I just screamed and Mama and I ran outside without even putting a shawl or a coat on. Papa and Sam got down, then they turned to help a young woman who was holding a baby all bundled up in her arms. A tall young man got down after her.

I wanted to run to her, but I was suddenly taken all over bashful. Could hardly believe this pretty lady was my big sister, and I was shy of that young man. Mama didn't hold back, though. Sarah started walking toward us through the snow and Mama just rushed at her. Hugged her so hard I thought baby Liza would be squashed. Then Sarah gave Liza over to Mama and held out her arms to me, and we just hugged and cried and hugged and cried.

Papa was standing there, smiling so hard it seemed his face would break.

Joseph, of course, tore out to see how Buck was and didn't even pay any attention to Sarah and her family. He was patting Buck all over, sure that the trip had been too much for the horse, but Buck looked just fine. Sam told him that the trip had livened Buck up no end. Anyway, Joseph spent the rest of the day out in the snow brushing Buck and feeding him oats and talking away a mile a minute to him. Buck's ears kept twitching, and honestly, it was hard to believe that horse wasn't talking back to him.

Joseph could hardly bear for Papa to take Buck back to the stables, and it was only when Papa pointed out that Buck would really rather spend the night in a warm stall than out in a snowy field that he agreed. Then of course *he* had to go, too.

We've been talking without hardly taking a pause for breath every waking hour since Sarah arrived. Sarah had to know all our story and we had to know hers. I'm going to write it all down, but it will have to wait until tomorrow. Baby Liza is crying and I'm going to go to her. It is surely the most wondrous thing in the world to hold her and just nuzzle my face down into her neck and smell her delicious baby smell. I love her to bits and pieces.

I already can't believe I was shy of Miles. He's just the nicest man I've ever met. He's so loving and kind with Sarah and the baby, and he treats Mama and Papa with respect. It will be like having another brother around.

Won't take Thomas's place, though.

Saturday, February 20ᵗʰ, 1864

Here's Sarah's story:

Sarah was sold off to another plantation owner way on the other side of the Great Dismal Swamp in North Carolina, but she says she determined to run off the first chance she got. The Missus was mean and the Master was meaner. She kept herself apart from the others, all except for one other girl about her own age. That girl knew someone who could put her in touch with a Conductor on the Underground Railroad, so Sarah did the same as we did, waited for a dark night with no moon, and then she ran.

She had pretty much the same kind of trip as us and by great good fortune, she ended up in Rochester, too. When she got there folks helped her settle in and then she met Miles. Miles was a free man and he had a good job. He helped Sarah get a job in an inn, washing dishes in the kitchen. Sarah wanted to keep out of sight as much as possible because of the Fugitive Slave Law. She was always worrying that some slave catcher would recognize her as a runaway and carry her back to Virginia. As the war went on, though, things got more and more confused. By last winter there were two Union army camps in Rochester, and with all the Northern soldiers around there she began to feel safer.

She and Miles got fonder and fonder of each other, then they finally married and she felt even more safe. She says she never passed one day without thinking of us, though, and wondering how we were. Then she found out she was going to have a baby of her own and she wanted to be with Mama so bad, it hurt.

When she told us that, she threw her arms around Mama and cried a bit. Mama cried, too.

My candle is guttering out. Best finish this story tomorrow.

Sunday, February, 21st, 1864

Father Miller welcomed Sarah and Miles and baby Liza into the church this morning. What a proud feeling it was to stand there beside them. "This is my sister, Sarah," I kept saying. "And my new brother, Miles. And," almost best of all, "my *niece* Liza."

Father Miller said a prayer for Thomas, too, and we all prayed that the war might end soon.

———————————

Now I'll get back to Sarah's story:

When baby Liza was born, Sarah began to pine even more for Mama and her family. Then one day Miles met a man named Holmes who had helped a family escape up to Canada. He mentioned our names and Miles realized the family he was talking about might be us. Miles got excited and brought the man home to meet Sarah. She asked him more questions, then knew for certain it was us. In that moment she determined they had to follow us up here.

Mister Holmes helped them, and they got on a Canada steamer the next week. It was easier for them than it was for us, because Miles was a free man and he had his free papers. Sarah didn't, but there was a lot of disorder around the harbour because of the war and all, and the slave catchers had pretty well given up by then, so they just held their heads high and walked onto that ship as bold as could be and nobody stopped them.

They were told that we were heading for Toronto, and Mister Holmes gave them Reverend Brown's name, so when they arrived they looked him up and he wrote to us. Sarah said she just about went crazy until she heard back that Papa was coming for her. She was so afraid we wouldn't get Reverend Brown's letter, or that we had moved on somewhere else.

Wednesday, February 24th, 1864

It is wonderful having Sarah and her family here with us. Joseph is getting to know Sarah now, and is more and more interested in baby Liza. He even asked Sarah if he could hold her today.

Monday, February 29th, 1864

It's a leap year. Means we get an extra day in February. The weather is so horrible I could certainly do without it.

Baby Liza has a cold and is fretful. She's crying all the time. The cabin is feeling awfully small and crowded. We're so happy to have Sarah and her family here that we're not complaining, but it's hard on Mama. Our baby is due in about a month and Mama's feeling a mite peaked. Sarah is a real help, though. She's taken over most of the washing and ironing. Joseph and I are still picking up and delivering the wash after school.

Tuesday, March 1st, 1864

They have a saying here in Canada: If March comes in like a lion it will go out like a lamb.

Well, today is certainly lion-like. The wind is howling around our little cabin and making its way in through every crack and cranny. We're keeping the fire up and trying to stay as warm as possible. Baby Liza is still fussing, though, and we're all getting fussed as well.

Friday, March 4ᵗʰ, 1864

Finally, the wind and snow and rain have stopped and the sun came out. It was the first day in a long time that it wasn't just pure misery going to school and back. Snow's going, but there's a lot of mud in its place. Some streets, you can't walk along them without sinking in up to your ankles.

Amelia came home with me after school to visit. She loves the baby and really likes to hold her. Luckily, Liza seems over her cold and was back to her usual smiley little self.

Missus Long and Noah came by, too. I think it made Missus Long sad to hold Liza, but she didn't say anything, just cuddled her. She brought over a cap and mittens that she had knitted herself. Noah brought over a rattle that he made. Turns out he's real good at carving.

Saturday, March 5ᵗʰ, 1864

Joseph pestered Mama all this morning to let him have a couple of pennies from the reward money she put away for him back in October. She finally gave in and he was off. He wouldn't tell anyone why he wanted them. When he got back he ran right over to the cradle where baby Liza was sleeping by the fire. He reached into his pocket and brought out a long string of licorice and gave it to her! Turns out he wanted to give her a present, too, and that was the best thing he could think of.

Sarah was real sweet. She thanked Joseph and said she'd put it away until Liza got some teeth to chew it with. Joseph was just beaming happy.

Tuesday, March 8*th*, 1864

Seems like life has gotten awfully busy lately. What with delivering and picking up laundry after school, and taking care of Liza while Sarah does the ironing, I am dog-tired when it comes bedtime. Hard to make myself write in this journal, but I am determined to keep at it.

We got good news today. I was down at the harbour after school with Sarah and baby Liza and Miles. Amelia and her daddy came walking along and stopped to talk to us. Captain Pearce turned to me. "Julia May," he said, "I don't rightly believe you were ever properly thanked for rescuing my daughter last fall."

I blushed and just muttered something. Couldn't even meet his eyes I was so embarrassed. Anyway, he went on to thank me nice as could be, and then asked to be introduced to Sarah and Miles. First thing I knew, he and Miles were talking away all about boats. Seems Miles has always wanted to sail on one. As they talked, and Captain Pearce was telling him stories about sailing on the lakes, Miles was getting more and more excited. Sounded more like a boy than a young man. Finally he just sort of blurted out, "Could I work for you, Captain Pearce? No need to pay me until I learn the ropes, but I'd dearly love a chance to go out on the lakes with you in the spring."

As Mama says, you could have knocked me over with a feather.

Captain Pearce sort of hemmed and hawed for a moment or two, then he smiled. "Fair enough," he said, and he laid his hand on my shoulder. "I do owe this family a favour. Tell you what. I'll take you out with me this spring after the breakup. If you learn fast enough, I'll sign you on as a regular deckhand by the end of summer. How does that sound?"

Miles could hardly answer him, he was so pleased. Sarah's not so sure about it, though. She doesn't like the idea of Miles being away so much, and she's worried about the dangers, but she knows jobs are hard to come by and this is a good chance for Miles.

Later on, when Amelia and I were by ourselves, she went on and on about how nice it was of her daddy to give Miles a chance at a job, but I just said Captain Pearce was lucky to be getting such a good man. For a moment there things got a mite testy, but we both realized it and stopped ourselves. We are too good friends to fight. It was horrible when we did. We don't want to do that again.

Friday, March 11th, 1864

Joseph and I went down to the harbour today after school. We had to pick up some washing at a lady's house near there and Joseph wanted to look at the ships. There are a lot of them in there, all frozen solid in the ice — sailing ships and lots of steamers — so many they're tied up side by side. The sailing ships are called schooners. I think that is the funniest word.

Saturday, March 19th, 1864

Liza is getting a tooth and she's fussing again. Seems like the only time she's happy is when Joseph is holding her! I can't believe how good he is with her. He's usually such a wild little boy, but when he's holding Liza he's quiet and gentle.

Monday, March 21st, 1864

Noah came by to tell me that his papa and brothers have come in from the lumber camp. The snow's pretty well gone and it's too muddy to get the logs out now. He's going up to their piece of land to help them clear brush and get ready for planting, then Missus Long is going up to join them and they'll be living there all the time. Noah said his papa felt real bad about Missus Long losing the baby. He wants to get a good shanty built before she goes up to join him, and Mama promised we'd take good care of her until then.

I won't hardly be seeing Noah any more at all now, only when they come in to town for supplies. I'm surprised at how bad I'm feeling about that.

Sunday, March 27th, 1864

Easter Sunday and the sun is shining. The snow is all gone and everything seems to be dripping and sparkling. Except for the mud. The mud is unbelievable.

Everyone in town was wearing their finest clothes for church this morning, but the ladies were having a hard time making their way down the streets. Even

Poulett Street was a muddy mess. Our church service was joyful, though. No one could be fussed on such a beautiful spring day.

Thursday, March 31ˢᵗ, 1864

Guess the old saying is true. It's the last day of March and March is going out like a lamb. It's actually warm! Joseph and I went down to the harbour after school again today and the river is just raging in and breaking up all the ice. The captains and their men are back on their boats and getting ready to leave. Miles is down on Captain Pearce's boat. He was working on the deck and smiling to beat the band when we saw him. He is one happy man.

Saturday, April 9ᵗʰ, 1864

Very exciting today. The ice was breaking up fast and the ships were all starting to leave. What a commotion! The steamers went out first, fighting their way through the remaining ice and sending it crashing against the shore. The schooners were the last to leave. Amelia came down to see her daddy and her brother William off, and she and Sarah just stood there watching the ship leave. They were holding each other's hand. Amelia has never told Sarah about when her daddy was missing last summer, but Sarah knows how dangerous sailing on the lakes can be.

Monday, April 11th, 1864

We had an uproar this afternoon. I came home from school and went to check on Liza, as usual. She wasn't in her cradle, so I found Sarah and asked her where Liza was.

"In her cradle, of course," Sarah said, but I told her she wasn't.

Well, Sarah near took a fit. Mama was lying down — our baby's due any day now — and she didn't know where the baby was, either. Then I looked out the kitchen window. There, in the field beside the house where Buck is, were Joseph and the baby. Liza can sit up pretty well now, and Joseph was holding her perched on the fence. She was patting Buck on the nose and looked like she was having a lovely time. I know how soft Buck's muzzle is, and I guess she loved it, too. Just as we saw them, Buck gave a nicker and shook his head.

Sarah ran out, screaming. I thought she was about to tear a strip off Joseph's hide. When she asked him why in the good Lord's name he had done such a thing he just said he thought Liza would like it.

And I guess he was right, because when Sarah snatched her off and carried her back up here to the house she cried something terrible.

Wednesday, April 13th, 1864

Our baby was born today! Mama let me name her Aleisha. She is BEAUTIFUL BEAUTIFUL BEAU-TIFUL!

Friday, April 15th, 1864

I can't stop carrying that baby around. But I will, just long enough to tell about how she was born.

We had just finished breakfast and I was getting ready to go to school when Mama suddenly sat down. She looked up at me and said, "Julia May, fetch Missus Robinson and then take Joseph down to the harbour to see the ships. The baby's coming."

Missus Robinson helps all the coloured ladies in town with their babies unless they have a problem and need a doctor. I have to admit, I panicked. I guess I was running around like a chicken with its head cut off, because Mama spoke to me again real sharp. "Do as I tell you, Julia May," she said. So I did. I ran to get

Joseph and dragged him to Missus Robinson's house. She gathered up her stuff and set off up the hill to our cabin.

"Keep that boy away for today," she said, "and tonight you'll have a new baby brother or sister."

I ran to the stables then, still dragging Joseph, and told Papa. He left right away to go back to the cabin, too. I remembered then how one of Mama's friends took me away for the day when Mama had Joseph. I was confused that day because when I came home there was a baby in the house. I didn't have the slightest notion of where it came from. Wasn't until a year or so later that Mama told me about babies and how they get here.

Anyway, I kept Joseph busy all day — never even thought of going to school. We watched the boats in the harbour, then went exploring along the river, then I even let Joseph do a little bit of climbing up in the rocks. Came the afternoon I was hungry and so was Joseph, so I figured it was time to go home.

Sure enough, when we went into the cabin Mama was resting beside the fire, holding our new baby. Joseph was astounded, but I can see he's going to be as silly-fond of her as he is of Liza.

Mama's calling . . . Will finish this later.

I'm sitting by the fire holding my new baby sister on my lap. Aleisha. It's hard to manage, but I want to write down what I'm feeling. I just have to let it out somehow. Mama is asleep in the bed beside me. Papa is sleeping in the chair by her side. Sarah is in the other room settling Liza. Joseph was finally persuaded to go to bed, so he's asleep, too. It's just me and Aleisha awake right now. She's looking up at me with big dark eyes. I have to laugh. She has that same stubborn, determined look on her face that Mama gets when she has her mind set on something. I wonder what Aleisha has her mind set on right now. Maybe figuring out who I am.

I have this warm, comfortable feeling spreading all through me. It's as though something is telling me that everything is going to be just fine now.

Thomas is going to come home to us, I know it.

And I pray that somewhere Caleb and Daniel have made good lives for themselves, too. Maybe after the war we'll find them. Maybe, if the North wins, we might even find other relatives.

In any case, we're a real family now, and this family is going to survive.

Epilogue

And survive, the family did, but not without difficulties. The American Civil War ended in April of 1865, just a year after Aleisha was born. Thomas finally returned to Canada, though he had been badly wounded in the war. He recovered from his wounds, but his war experiences were so horrific he never wanted to talk about them. He said it was enough that the North had won and that from then on all people of colour were free in the South as well as the North.

Racial prejudice dies hard, however, and by the time Thomas got back to Owen Sound, jobs for Black people were hard to come by. Thomas was forced to leave home yet again and make his way to Toronto, where he was fortunate enough to find a job working as a waiter in a restaurant.

Julia May and Noah were married when they were both still quite young. They lived with Noah's parents and helped them on their farm after Noah's two elder brothers also left for jobs in larger towns. They eventually took over the farm when Noah's parents died. They had five children.

Julia May was never able to achieve her ambition of becoming a teacher, but she finished high school and made certain that all of her five children did as well. She and Noah attended every one of their graduations with enormous pride. Julia May was delighted to see one of her granddaughters finally become a teacher, even though that young woman had to teach in a small segregated Black country school. Ontario, as Canada West came to be called, was not yet ready for Black teachers to work in the integrated schools.

Amelia married a young man who eventually became a successful doctor in Owen Sound. She and Julia May remained good friends for the rest of their lives. They visited back and forth in each other's homes, sometimes raising the eyebrows of neighbours who would walk into Amelia's rather formal home and find her chatting and sharing a cup of coffee with Julia May. Many people still believed that Blacks should know their place and keep to it, and "their place" was not sitting at the dining room table of a white woman.

Sarah and Miles stayed in Owen Sound and had three more children. Miles worked on the ships until he was quite old, surviving the dangers of the sailing life and even one shipwreck, much to Sarah's relief.

To his family's dismay, Joseph's spirited disposition did not fit well with schoolwork, and he was only too glad to leave school as soon as he could. For a while he drifted, unsure as to where his future lay, but he never lost his uncanny ability with animals and continued to work with horses whenever and wherever he got the chance. Eventually his talent was brought to the notice of the owner of a stable of thoroughbred horses, and he was hired on. He proved successful in this endeavour, and married a young woman whom the townsfolk called a tomboy. Together they raised four children, all equally lively and all equally obsessed with horses.

Julia May's mother, with Sarah and Miles's help, was finally able to purchase her sewing machine. She eventually became one of the best seamstresses in Owen Sound. As they grew older, Aleisha and Liza helped her and, finally, the three women set up their own business. Aleisha and Liza expanded the enterprise and made ladies' hats as well. They were much sought after for special occasions.

Julia May's parents never lost hope of finding Caleb and Daniel after the war ended, but unfortunately they never did. However, they and Julia May took solace in the thought that wherever they were, if

Caleb and Daniel were still alive, they were free men.

They did not find any of their other missing relatives, either, but years later a great-great-niece of Julia May, a teacher who lived and taught in Pennsylvania in the United States, attended a genealogical conference in the town of Durham, in Ontario, Canada. She was pleased and proud to be able to trace her roots back to Julia May Jackson in Owen Sound, through Julia May's long-lost older brother, Caleb.

Historical Note

In the eighteenth century, during the British colonial period in North America, all the colonies, including those in Canada, had slaves. Most of them had been brought over from Africa — kidnapped from their villages, wrenched from their families, and forced onto squalid slave ships to be sold in slave markets in the New World. It was not until 1807 that Parliament abolished the British slave trade and it became illegal to carry slaves in British ships, and it was not until 1833 that slavery was finally abolished in the entire British Empire, including Canada.

After the American War of Independence (1775–1783), a movement to end slavery began to grow throughout the North. Not all of the northerners were against slavery, and some Northern states still had a few slaves right through the 1850s, but many did look upon slavery as not in keeping with Christianity and with moral values. Indeed, it was strongly held by some that slavery corrupted whites because of the power they held over enslaved people, at the same time as it oppressed and abused Africans in America.

Abolitionist societies were formed that advocated strongly for the cessation of this exploitative practice.

Slavery continued to flourish in the South, however. The large plantation owners and wealthy farmers growing indigo, rice, tobacco and cotton referred to slavery as the South's "peculiar institution," and insisted that slave labour was necessary to harvest their crops. In a speech to Congress on February 6, 1837, John C. Calhoun, a senator from South Carolina who also served as vice-president of the United States from March 4, 1825 to December 28, 1832, affirmed that slavery was actually a "positive good" and gave the slaves the benefit of white supervision and instruction. This became one of the justifications for slavery, countering the work of the abolitionists.

President Abraham Lincoln, a Republican, was elected in 1860. His name was not included on the ballots of most Southern states, however, and thus his election split the nation. Slave owners in the South feared that the intent of the Republicans was the abolition of slavery in their states. This, along with other factors, led to the South seceding from the Union, and the onset of the American Civil War (1861–1865).

Not long after the war broke out, three slaves escaped from their master and sought refuge at

Fortress Monroe, a Union Army fort in Virginia. The commander of the fort was General Benjamin F. Butler, a lawyer by profession. The slaves' master followed them into the fort and demanded their return. General Butler, however, refused to return the men into slavery. As slaves were considered to be *property* in the South, not *humans,* and under the strict laws of nations all the property of an enemy may be seized in time of war, General Butler declared that these men could be considered "Contrabands of War." He ruled that it was not legally necessary to return them to their masters, despite the Fugitive Slave Law that had been passed in 1850. (This was a law that made it mandatory for citizens of Northern states to return escaped slaves to their owners in the South, even though slavery was not legal in those Northern states.)

Butler's decision established a precedent and opened the door wide for hundreds if not thousands of escaped slaves to seek refuge in the fort. Eventually there were so many that they could not be accommodated within the fortress walls, so camps were set up outside for them. Here they were given food and shelter and could work.

President Lincoln issued the first Emancipation Proclamation in September 1862, declaring the freedom of all slaves in any state of the Confederate States of America that did not return to Union control by January 1, 1863. The second order, issued January 1, 1863, named the specific states where it applied. On July 17, 1862, Congress passed two acts allowing the enlistment of African Americans in the Union Army, but official enrolment occurred only after the issuance of the first Proclamation. With President Abraham Lincoln's issuance of the second Emancipation Proclamation in 1863, the Civil War became a war to save the Union and to abolish slavery.

Close to 180,000 African Americans, comprising 163 units, served in the Union Army during the Civil War; African Americans also served in the Union Navy. Both free men and runaway slaves joined the fight, distinguishing themselves in numerous battles. Civil War losses were extremely high — more American military personnel died, from injuries and illness, in the Civil War than have died in all wars since that time in which American troops have fought. However, the death rate among African Americans was even higher than the average — over twenty percent of those enrolled in the Union Army during the Civil War lost their lives.

With the victory of the North at the end of the war,

all slaves in the United States obtained their freedom. Before this, however, the lives of most slaves on plantations in the Southern states had been unbelievably harsh, although slaves who lived in cities and towns often had easier lives and in some states were even allowed to learn to read and write. Many slaves lived in abject poverty, often half starved, and were worked almost beyond human endurance. They were whipped for attending prayer meetings, whipped for congregating in groups, whipped for having the audacity to learn to read and write, whipped for slipping away from their master's plantation to visit a spouse or ailing parent. Sometimes they were whipped to death. Husbands were sold away from wives. Children were wrenched from their mothers' arms and sold off, often never to see their parents again.

Even slight disobedience might be severely punished. Those who tried to escape and failed were subject to inhuman punishment, mutilation, shackling with chains, and often, death. Sometimes they were branded with hot irons. Still, many slaves became desperate enough to try to escape. Their aim was to get to the Northern states (where slavery had largely been abolished, starting just after the American War of Independence).

Even enslaved people whose owners were not purposefully cruel were never safe. Although a very few masters or mistresses did leave wills that set their slaves free, the vast majority willed their slaves to relatives, or left them to be sold off with the rest of their possessions to whoever wanted to buy them, without regard to the breaking up of families — even if those families had been together for years. These slaves could then find themselves in as harsh and as cruel conditions as all the rest, or even sold south to the cotton fields and be lost to their families forever. Many who had served their masters faithfully for years fared no better. When they grew too old to be of service they were often sold off to slave traders for whatever they could fetch.

Over the years, slaves found many ways to escape to freedom. Some got away by themselves. Others were able to secure false passes giving them "permission" from their masters to travel, or forged papers indicating that they had been freed. Quakers, a peaceful religious group that did not believe in slavery, helped slaves escape as early as the 1790s in Pennsylvania. There are many accounts handed down to us of brave and resourceful people — Black and white — who assisted fugitives on their way to the Northern states and even to Canada.

An organization arose that came to be called the Underground Railroad. This was not a railroad in the sense that we know it now, but rather a system of safe houses whose owners, both Black and white, would shelter escaping slaves and give them all the help they could. They adopted the language of the newest technological marvel of the age — the railroad — as a code to describe their secret and very dangerous activities. The people who guided escaping slaves along this railroad were called Conductors. An owl hoot, a bird call, a whistle or a whisper in the dead of night was often the signal that a Conductor was waiting to lead a slave to safety.

Some Conductors, such as Harriet Tubman, were slaves who had escaped and then deliberately returned and put themselves back in danger in order to help others escape as well. Those who helped the escaping slaves were very brave. Black Conductors could suffer the same penalties as the slaves themselves — whipping or death. White people who gave refuge to slaves faced the fury of their neighbours, reprisals, imprisonment, heavy fines and loss of property. Even in the free states of the North, the penalty for a white person who broke the Fugitive Slave Law and assisted an escaped slave, or failed to return a slave to his or her master, was a fine of a thousand dollars (which would be around eighteen thousand dollars today) and imprisonment.

Because the Fugitive Slave Law forced people in the Northern states to return escaped slaves to their owners if their owners or hired slave catchers could find them, many slaves decided to escape farther north, out of the United States, and up to Canada. There were many songs that told the stories of these escapes, it is said; some even gave instructions by incorporating secret information into the words of the songs. One of the most well-known was the direction to follow the North Star. This was included in the song "Follow the Drinking Gourd." Other signs, like the hanging of a quilt over the line outside a house, a candle in the window, or a lantern set outside, might indicate a safe house or "station."

Slaves escaped into Canada by various means. Some were boated across rivers, others were hidden on steamboats plying the waters between the United States and Canada. Once on Canadian shores the fugitives were free, although slave catchers did sometimes cross the border after them. Canadian law would not allow the slave catchers to take slaves back, but there was always danger even so, and a few people who had made it safely to Canada were even kidnapped and returned to the American South.

There were many communities of escaped slaves in Canada. One of the most prosperous was in Toronto, composed of escaped slaves and free Blacks. Some of the latter were descendents of slaves formerly held by the British in the early years, when Toronto was known as the Town of York. That community included business men and women, two doctors and other professionals. Toronto schools, like schools in Owen Sound, were not segregated, but all of the teachers were white. Only small segregated country schools hired Black teachers. Wilson Brooks, an RCAF Veteran, became Toronto's first Black schoolteacher, and later principal, in an integrated school in 1952. Segregated schools existed in Ontario until 1965.

The women of the Toronto Black community banded together to give help to newly arrived escaped slaves, while the Black churches also gave support. Even so, many fugitives did not feel safe so near the American border, and made their way farther inland. Some settled on farm land along the Durham Road; others made their way to Collingwood and on up to Owen Sound. Owen Sound was the northern terminus of the Underground Railroad. By 1872 over six hundred people of African origin lived there — almost ten percent of the town's total population.

Black citizens opened businesses in Owen Sound. The town was welcoming, but not without prejudice. Some of these businesses succeeded, others did not. Black men found jobs on ships plying the Great Lakes waters, in lumber camps and in the limestone quarries but, in general, there were few jobs for men or women, so many had to leave to seek their fortunes in larger cities. Many stayed, however, and raised their families in the town. To this day there is a lively Black community in Owen Sound. The Annual Emancipation Day Picnic has continued uninterrupted since 1862, and is still a cherished tradition. It grows bigger every year.

Characters in the story who are real people:

In Toronto:
Mr. George Blunt
Mrs. Teakle
Dr. Abbott

In Owen Sound:

Mr. and Mrs. John Frost of Sheldon Place

Old Man Henson (James Henson, born as Charley Chance; he changed his name on becoming a free man in the 1840s)

Father Thomas Henry Miller

Catherine Sutton (Nahneebahweequay)

Granny Taylor (Mary Taylor)

John "Daddy" Hall (1783–1900; credited with being the first Black settler in the fledgling settlement of Sydenham, later called Owen Sound)

Slaves lived in cabins on the plantation, though some "house slaves" were required to sleep over at the Big House in case their masters or mistresses needed them during the night. Family members could be sold off at the master's sole discretion.

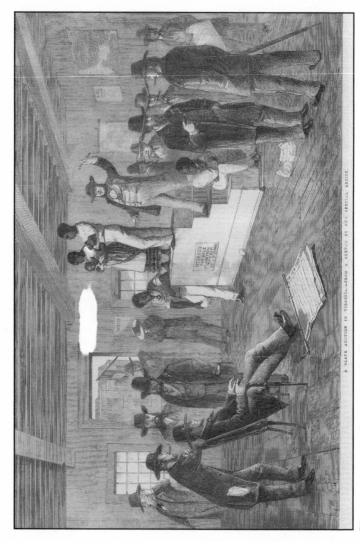

A SLAVE AUCTION IN VIRGINIA.—FROM A SKETCH BY OUR SPECIAL ARTIST.

Slaves were routinely auctioned off. Legally, they were property.

The list above, from Richmond, Virginia, in the 1860s, shows prices for men, women and child slaves. A girl "4 feet" high would sell for $450 to $475, a young woman $1125 to $1175.

Runaways (above) sometimes made for the Great Dismal Swamp near the Atlantic coast, searching for a place to hide. Escapees had to be on constant lookout for slave catchers (below), who operated even in states where escaped slaves were now living as free people.

OPERATIONS OF THE FUGITIVE-SLAVE LAW.

Slavery—U.S.

N. Y. PUBLIC LIBRARY
PICTURE COLLECTION

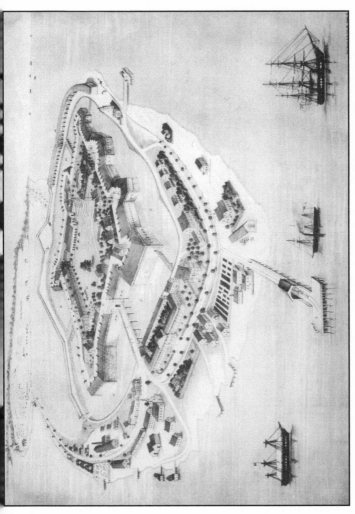

Escaped slaves often made their way to the Grand Contraband Camp at Fortress Monroe, built on a spit of land stretching into the Atlantic Ocean off southeastern Virginia.

The Queen's Hotel in Toronto was a favourite place to stay for Southerners and their families who had fled the turmoil of the Civil War.

TO COLORED MEN!

FREEDOM,

Protection, Pay, and a Call to Military Duty!

On the 1st day of January, 1863, the President of the United States proclaimed FREE-DOM to over THREE MILLIONS OF SLAVES. This decree is to be enforced by all the power of the Nation. On the 21st of July last he issued the following order:

PROTECTION OF COLORED TROOPS.

"WAR DEPARTMENT, ADJUTANT GENERAL'S OFFICE,
WASHINGTON, July 21.

"*General Order,* No. 233.

"The following order of the President is published for the information and government of all concerned:—

EXECUTIVE MANSION, WASHINGTON, July 30.

"'It is the duty of every Government to give protection to its citizens, of whatever class, color, or condition, and especially to those who are duly organized as soldiers in the public service. The law of nations, and the usages and customs of war, as carried on by civilized powers, permit no distinction as to color in the treatment of prisoners of war as public enemies. To sell or enslave any captured person on account of his color, is a relapse into barbarism, and a crime against the civilization of the age.

"'The Government of the United States will give the same protection to all its soldiers, and if the enemy shall sell or enslave any one because of his color, the offense shall be punished by retaliation upon the enemy's prisoners in our possession. It is, therefore, ordered, for every soldier of the United States, killed in violation of the laws of war, a rebel soldier shall be executed; and for every one enslaved by the enemy, or sold into slavery, a rebel soldier shall be placed at hard labor on the public works, and continued at such labor until the other shall be released and receive the treatment due to prisoners of war.

"'ABRAHAM LINCOLN.'"

"'By order of the Secretary of War.

"'E. D. TOWNSEND, Assistant Adjutant General.'"

That the President is in earnest the rebels soon began to find out, as witness the following order from his Secretary of War:

"WAR DEPARTMENT, WASHINGTON CITY, August 8, 1863.

"SIR: Your letter of the 3d inst., calling the attention of this Department to the cases of Orin H. Brown, William H. Johnston, and Wm. Wilson, three colored men captured on the gunboat Isaac Smith, has received consideration. This Department has directed that three rebel prisoners of South Carolina, if there be any such in our possession, and if not, three others, be confined in close custody and held as hostages for Brown, Johnston and Wilson, and that the fact be communicated to the rebel authorities at Richmond.

"Very respectfully your obedient servant,

"EDWIN M. STANTON, Secretary of War.

"The Hon. GIDEON WELLES, Secretary of the Navy."

And retaliation will be our practice now—man for man—to the bitter end.

LETTER OF CHARLES SUMNER,

Written with reference to the Convention held at Poughkeepsie, July 15th and 16th, 1863, to promote Colored Enlistments.

BOSTON, July 13th, 1863.

"I doubt if, in times past, our country could have expected from colored men any patriotic service. Such service is the return for protection. But now that protection has begun, the service should begin also. Nor should relative rights and duties be weighed with nicety. It is enough that our country, aroused at last to a sense of justice, seeks to enrol colored men among its defenders.

"If my counsels should reach such persons, I would say: enlist at once. Now is the day and now is the hour. Help to overcome your cruel enemies now battling against your country, and in this way you will surely overcome those other enemies hardly less cruel, here at home, who will still seek to degrade you. This is not the time to hesitate or to higgle. Do your duty to our country, and you will set an example of generous self-sacrifice which will conquer prejudice and open all hearts.

"Very faithfully yours,

"CHARLES SUMNER."

This broadsheet announced U.S. President Abraham Lincoln's freeing of three million slaves. It urged African American men to join the Union Army in fighting the South.

The 54th Massachusetts "Colored" Regiment is shown fighting
Confederate soldiers at Fort Wagner, South Carolina.

John and Mary Frost of Sheldon Place built cabins for escapees on their 101-acre property, and helped them out with food and jobs. The building still stands overlooking Owen Sound.

John "Daddy" Hall was born a free Black in Amherstburg, Canada West, but he and most of his family were kidnapped by slave traders and sold to a plantation owner in Kentucky. Daddy Hall escaped back to Canada via the Underground Railroad. He is credited with being the first Black settler in the fledgling settlement of Sydenham, later called Owen Sound.

Father Thomas Henry Miller was a lay preacher for the British Methodist Episcopal Church (below) in Owen Sound.

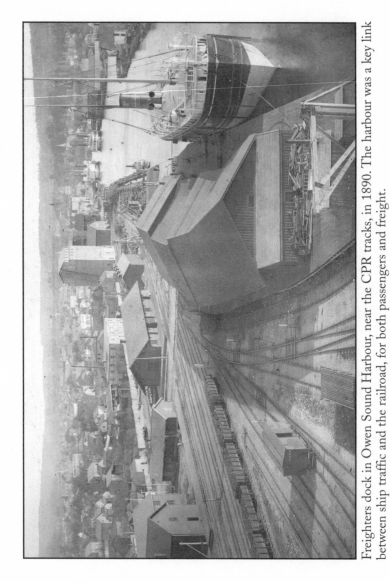

Freighters dock in Owen Sound Harbour, near the CPR tracks, in 1890. The harbour was a key link between ship traffic and the railroad, for both passengers and freight.

Children pose for a photograph in front of a school in Owen Sound in the early 1900s.

The West Rocks are part of the Niagara Escarpment that stretches from Niagara Falls through the Bruce Peninsula to Manitoulin Island.

Follow the Drinking Gourd

When the sun comes back,
and the first quail calls,
Follow the drinking gourd,
For the old man is waiting
for to carry you to freedom
If you follow the drinking gourd.

Chorus:
Follow the drinking gourd,
Follow the drinking gourd,
For the old man is waiting
for to carry you to freedom
If you follow the drinking gourd.

The riverbank will make a very good road,
The dead trees show you the way.
Left foot, peg foot traveling on,
Following the drinking gourd.

The river ends between two hills,
Follow the drinking gourd,
There's another river on the other side,
Follow the drinking gourd.

When the great big river meets the little river,
Follow the drinking gourd.
For the old man is waiting
for to carry you to freedom
If you follow the drinking gourd.

Virginia Cornbread

Three cups of corn meal, one cup of flour,
one tablespoonful of sugar, one teaspoonful
of salt, two heaping teaspoonfuls of baking
powder, one tablespoonful of lard, three cups
of milk and three eggs.

Mix together the flour, corn meal, sugar,
salt and baking powder; rub in the lard cold,
add the eggs well beaten, then the milk. Pour
into a greased iron pot or skillet. Bake on the
hearth covered in coals or in a hot oven until
firm.

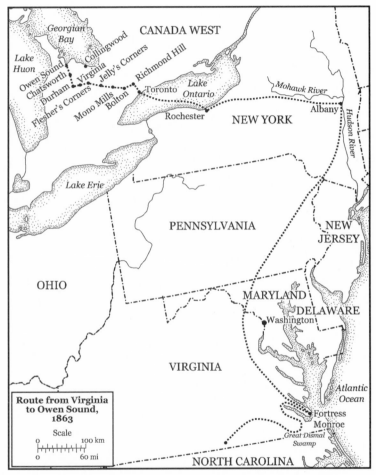

The route from southern Virginia to Fortress Monroe, north to
Albany and across Lake Ontario, is one that many fugitives took
while fleeing north to Canada West on the Underground Railroad.
The Jacksons followed another typical route northwest from
Toronto to Owen Sound.

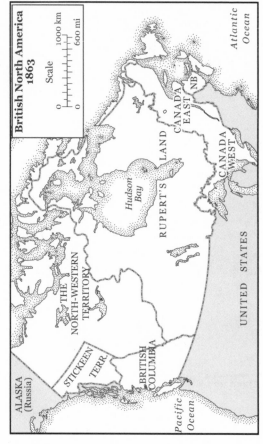

British North America, including Canada West and Canada East, in 1863.

Acknowledgments

Grateful acknowledgment is made for permission to reprint the following:

Cover portrait: Bazoline Estelle Usher, Library of Congress, LC-USZ6-2231.
Cover background: Detail from *The Underground Railroad*, Charles T. Webber, Cincinnati Art Museum, Subscription Fund Purchase, Accession #: 1927.26.

Page 215: *Row of slave cabins on a southern plantation, 1800s;* hand-colored woodcut, North Wind Picture Archives, SOCI3A-00179.
Page 216: "A Slave Auction in Virginia," *Illustrated London News,* February 16, 1861, courtesy of the Division of Rare and Manuscript Collections, Cornell University Library.
Page 217: *Slave Dealer's Price Listing. Richmond, Virginia:* Johnson, Snyder and Adams, September 20, 1860, courtesy of the Division of Rare and Manuscript Collections, Cornell University Library.
Page 218 (upper): *Slaves escaping to the North through southern swamps during US Civil War;* woodcut, North Wind Picture Archives, SOCI3A-00080.
Page 218 (lower): *Operations of the fugitive-slave law,* Picture Collection, The New York Public Library, Astor, Lenox and Tilden Foundations, 807834.
Page 219: *Fortress Monroe, February 1862,* Ferdinand Mayer & Co., Lithographers.
Page 220: *Advertisement for Queen's Hotel,* Statistics Canada, *The Canada Year Book, 1874.*
Page 221: D135 CT 1863; Colored Troop Div. Letters Received; Record Group 94; National Archives & Record Administration, Washington, DC.

Page 222: *54th Massachusetts (black) Regiment assaulting Confederate stronghold at Fort Wagner, SC,* North Wind Picture Archives, EVCW3A-00063.

Page 223: 333 4th Avenue East, Sheldon Place, The Grey Roots Archival Collection, PF49S14F28I3.

Page 224: *John "Daddy" Hall,* The Grey Roots Archival Collection 1976.020.019.

Page 225 (upper): *Father William Miller* [Father Thomas Henry Miller], The Grey Roots Archival Collection, 1968.061.016.

Page 225 (lower): *BME Church, Owen Sound,* The Grey Roots Archival Collection A2006.070.001.

Page 226: *Owen Sound harbour (S.S.* Alberta *in port; CPR tracks),* The Grey Roots Archival Collection 1980.273.001.

Page 227: Unidentified school group, The Grey Roots Archival Collection A2006.073.082.

Page 228: West Rocks, courtesy of George Kraemer.

Pages 231–232: Maps by Paul Heersink/Paperglyphs. Map data © 2002 Government of Canada with permission from Natural Resources Canada.

Thanks to Greg McKinnon, Toronto District School Board Archivist, for routing us to the research of Joel Weiss and Robert S. Brown, which provided helpful information on the duration and timing of the school years in Toronto and elsewhere in the 1860s.

For Jan Andrews
and
Rachna Gilmore

I would like to thank Lawrence Hill, author of *The Book of Negroes,* for his support and encouragement, and for his careful reading of the manuscript in its early stages. I would also like to thank Dr. Karolyn Smardz Frost, author of *I've Got a Home in Glory Land,* for her advice and expertise, and Barbara Hehner for her meticulous fact-checking.

Thanks, also, to Diane Kerner and to Sandy Bogart Johnston, who guided and pushed me into writing the best book I possibly could. Sandy is the heart and soul of the Dear Canada books, and she works as hard on them as do the authors.

My gratitude to Bonita Johnson de Matteis and Terri Jackson for their help in finding information about the early Black community in Owen Sound; Mary Smith and Mindy Gill-Sitoski at the Owen Sound Marine & Rail Museum; Trevor Parsons, Amelia Ferguson and Karin Foster at the Grey Roots Museum & Archives; Judy Armstrong, Beth Hall and Margaret Hodgins at the Owen Sound and North Grey Union Public Library; and John Shragge, The Road Scholar, Ontario.

About the Author

Karleen Bradford's ties to Owen Sound are strong. Her father was born and brought up there, as was her husband. Her parents met in Owen Sound, and Karleen met *her* husband there. It was only natural, then, that when Karleen's husband retired, they would return from a number of overseas postings to live in Owen Sound.

After moving back, Karleen began learning more about the African Canadian community in the city and exploring its history as a terminus of the Underground Railroad. Her uncle was ninety-two by then, and she spent many hours listening to stories of his youth. One story was of his mother Bessie Scott's friendship with a young woman named Julia Miller. Julia was the daughter of slaves who had escaped on the Underground Railroad and eventually settled in Canada. Karleen's uncle told of how shocked some of Bessie's neighbours were when they would drop in for a visit and find her and Julia sharing a cup of coffee at the dining room table. Although escaped slaves were originally welcomed into the city, racism had soon raised its head when jobs became scarce for all the men there.

To learn more about the Underground Railroad connection, Karleen attended a Black History Conference in the nearby town of Durham, Ontario. Many attendees at this conference were African Americans who had come north to try and trace ancestors who had fled to Canada to escape slavery. "At this conference," Karleen says, "I found myself sitting beside a woman from Pennsylvania who had come up to search for information about her great-great-aunt. That great-great-aunt turned out to be the very person who had befriended my grandmother."

Karleen was able to tell the woman the story of the friendship between Julia Miller and Bessie Scott. Never much of a believer in coincidences, this "chance" meeting convinced Karleen that she was meant to write about the courageous people who had faced such terrible hardships to find freedom in Canada, and this book was born.

Many of its characters are historical people. Karleen's great-aunt, Emma Scott Nasmith, knew Father Miller when she was a child. She wrote an essay which has been reprinted in *Northern Terminus:*

The African Canadian History Journal, vol.4/2007. In this essay Emma Scott Nasmith recounts her memories of Saturday afternoons when she and her friends were free to play and explore the meadows, the high rocks and the caves surrounding the city. If they tarried too long they were often found by Father Miller, who gently hurried them on their way home. She speaks lovingly of what a kind man he was.

Karleen was writing the final drafts of this book during the 2008 electoral campaign in the United States. "I was writing about a time when African Americans were enslaved, beaten, tortured and murdered," she says. "When they were not even considered to be human, but property. Who could ever have imagined that less than a hundred and fifty years later an African American would become President of the United States?"

Karleen Bradford is the award-winning author of twenty-four works of fiction and non-fiction for children and adults. Her many historical novels include *With Nothing But Our Courage* in the Dear Canada series; *The Nine Days Queen;* and a series of five novels about the crusades, including *There Will Be Wolves,* which won the CLA Best Young Adult Novel Award. She has also won the Saskatchewan Young Readers'

Choice Shining Willow Award, and the Max and Greta Ebel Award. Karleen's *Shadows on a Sword* was nominated for the Geoffrey Bilson Award for Historical Fiction, as was *Angeline*. Her books have also been nominated for the Silver Birch Award, the Red Maple Award, and several other readers' choice awards. In 2006 she won the Allan Sangster Award for outstanding dedication and service to the Canadian Authors Association.

Library and Archives Canada Cataloguing in Publication

Bradford, Karleen
A desperate road to freedom : the underground railroad
diary of Julia May Jackson / Karleen Bradford.

(Dear Canada)
ISBN 978-0-545-99619-8

1. Underground Railroad--Juvenile fiction. 2. Fugitive
slaves--Canada--Juvenile fiction. 3. Fugitive slaves--United
States--Juvenile fiction. 4. Canada--Race relations--Juvenile
fiction. I. Title. II. Series: Dear Canada

PS8553.R217D48 2009   jC813'.54   C2009-901152-2

ISBN 10 0-545-99619-8

6 5 4 3 2 1   Printed in Canada   09 10 11 12 13

The display type was set in Centaur.
The text was set in Caslon.

First printing June 2009

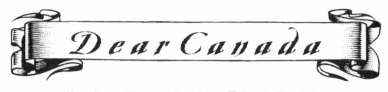

Dear Canada

Where the River Takes Me, The Hudson's Bay Company Diary of Jenna Sinclair by Julie Lawson

Whispers of War, The War of 1812 Diary of Susanna Merritt by Kit Pearson

Winter of Peril, The Newfoundland Diary of Sophie Loveridge by Jan Andrews

With Nothing But Our Courage, The Loyalist Diary of Mary MacDonald by Karleen Bradford

Go to www.scholastic.ca/dearcanada for information on the Dear Canada Series — see inside the books, read an excerpt or a review, post a review, and more.

Judith Proulx
Physio Sports Plus
Place Orleans Blvd.

Physiotherapist
with Scott Raworda